W9-AXL-386

It was hard to reveal this side of himself to Ellery.

Hard to know that he *needed* this dog.

"You're doing great." Ellery's focus was on Behr, but Margo's tail wagged as if the compliment had been directed to her.

They both laughed, and the tension dissipated like a deployment care package.

"You, too, girl." Ellery offered the dog a treat. "Do you want me to put the balance harness on her so you can feel what it's like?" she asked Behr.

He gave one determined nod.

Ellery strode over to the storage cabinets that lined the back wall. She returned with the harness and knelt, sliding it on Margo. Behr probably should have been watching how to do the same, but right now he was concentrating on standing next to Margo and not having his knees liquefy.

Ellery stood. "See what you think."

Behr gripped the handle, his knuckles turning white. The handle was the right height, and it did make him feel sturdy. Supported.

Like the woman beaming at him from the other side of the dog.

Jill Lynn pens stories filled with humor, faith and happily-ever-afters. She's an ACFW Carol Award–winning author and has a bachelor's degree in communications from Bethel University. An avid fan of thrift stores, summer and coffee, she lives in Colorado with her husband and two children, who make her laugh on a daily basis. Connect with her at jill-lynn.com.

Books by Jill Lynn

Love Inspired

K-9 Companions

The Veteran's Vow

Colorado Grooms

The Rancher's Surprise Daughter
The Rancher's Unexpected Baby
The Bull Rider's Secret
Her Hidden Hope
Raising Honor
Choosing His Family

Falling for Texas
Her Texas Family
Her Texas Cowboy

Visit the Author Profile page at LoveInspired.com for more titles.

The Veteran's Vow

Jill Lynn

LOVE INSPIRED

INSPIRATIONAL ROMANCE

If you purchased this book without a cover you should be aware that this book is stolen property. It was reported as "unsold and destroyed" to the publisher, and neither the author nor the publisher has received any payment for this "stripped book."

LOVE INSPIRED®
INSPIRATIONAL ROMANCE

Recycling programs for this product may not exist in your area.

ISBN-13: 978-1-335-56756-7

The Veteran's Vow

Copyright © 2022 by Jill Buteyn

All rights reserved. No part of this book may be used or reproduced in any manner whatsoever without written permission except in the case of brief quotations embodied in critical articles and reviews.

This is a work of fiction. Names, characters, places and incidents are either the product of the author's imagination or are used fictitiously. Any resemblance to actual persons, living or dead, businesses, companies, events or locales is entirely coincidental.

This edition published by arrangement with Harlequin Books S.A.

For questions and comments about the quality of this book, please contact us at CustomerService@Harlequin.com.

Love Inspired
22 Adelaide St. West, 41st Floor
Toronto, Ontario M5H 4E3, Canada
www.LoveInspired.com

Printed in U.S.A.

God is our refuge and strength,
a very present help in trouble.
—*Psalm* 46:1

Shana and Rachelle—thank you for making this book possible. You're the best dream team a girl could ask for.

Terry—thank you for always being my support.

S & L—thanks for letting me write books *and* be your mom. I'm so very proud of you. Love you so much!

And to the men and women who have served and the families who love and support them— thank you, thank you. This one's for you.

Chapter One

Ellery Watson's job description did not include tracking down veterans at their homes to investigate why they hadn't shown up for training, but when she realized her no-show lived in her town, she'd been unable to resist.

The waiting list for a service dog from Helping Paws was lengthy, so it was rare to inconceivable for someone to not jump at the opportunity when it came along. Why, she wondered, would someone miss out on their chance for physical and emotional assistance once they were finally matched with a canine companion?

As the person who spent copious hours pairing the right dog to the right veteran and made very little money doing it, Ellery would *love* to know the answer to that question.

She turned off Evergreen Street and into the Mt. Vista condominium parking lot, and chose a spot in front of unit G, which was a ground-floor walk-up. Fitting, based on the medical reasons outlined in the man's application.

Her stomach gave a twist of unease as she parked and turned off the engine, communicating that this might not be the smartest thing she'd ever done. Usually veterans came to the training center on her property—a fancy term for a detached, oversize garage that had been converted into a space to host group sessions.

Helping Paws was grassroots. No swanky buildings. No offices outside of the one that had taken over her basement. Though they did have a catchy logo thanks to one of the volunteers being versed in graphic design.

Ellery stepped out of her vehicle and gave the signal for her Siberian husky to follow. Dash leaped from the seat to the parking lot with agility. He wasn't a trained service dog because his demeanor was too aloof. Stores, gatherings, people in general—he didn't do well with any of those things. He preferred Ellery or no one, and he was perfectly happy sniffing around the backyard alone. He reminded Ellery of a crotchety senior even though he was only four years old. Despite his introversion, Dash was content to go where she went—as long as she kept him away from crowds.

One of the many things Ellery had learned

since she'd begun working with veterans was to not surprise them, so she slammed the driver's door shut with extra oomph to signal her arrival.

Dash glued himself to her left side, and she started a running commentary with him in the interest of continuing to announce her presence.

"You're a good boy, aren't you, buddy?"

His tail wagged in response.

"Why in the world would anyone not want a dog as great as you, huh?"

Dash glanced away as if it was impossible to answer that question.

"Exactly." Ellery directed Dash to sit in the patch of grass between the parking lot and the sidewalk and then knocked on the plastic frame of the screen door. She was almost certain she heard shuffling inside, but no one answered.

She repeated the knock with more force. "Hello? I'm from Helping Paws. I'm here about your service dog."

Still nothing. Ellery had half a mind to plunk down on the entry step and wait this guy out. She raised her fist to knock one more time, but the inside door swung open before she could complete the motion. Her hand dropped back to her side.

The man behind the screen door was fit and trim, with a light beard and olive skin. He wore a gray athletic T-shirt and black exercise pants, and his inquisitive caramel eyes questioned the reason for her presence.

"Hi, I'm here about—"

"Heard you yelling. No need to repeat."

Yelling might be exaggerating a bit. "Okay, great. Well, I'm Ellery Watson." *And you're Behr Delgado, who didn't show up for training today.* "I wanted to make sure you got the info since you missed the first training. I wouldn't normally drop by like this, but I couldn't get ahold of you by phone." She'd left two messages and emailed him three times in the week leading up to training. But even with his lack of reply, she'd still assumed he would show this morning, because it made no sense for him not to. "Since we live in the same town—the charity is located here in Mt. Vista—I thought I'd stop by on my way home from work."

Kind of a stretch since her office was at her house. But she'd been out delivering supplies to one of her veterans who lived about twenty minutes away, so it was somewhat the truth.

Ellery had needed to decompress after a long day of training her newest group of veterans—the group Behr was scheduled to be part of—and a drive with her favorite playlist had provided that for her.

"I don't need a dog. Sorry." His voice held a

hint of apology and a heap of certainty. "The application was a mistake. I never applied for one."

"Someone did."

"Yep. Just not me." He stayed behind the screen door, his arms crossed over a chest that said either he still lifted, or he hadn't lost the physique he'd gained in the military.

Ellery's brother, Ace, had been lanky. Wiry. Like a straw with glasses and a shaved head due to his fading hairline that had begun in his early twenties. He'd teased Ellery about making up for her height—five foot five *and a half*—with spunk.

Spunky Brewster, he'd called her.

But Behr was solid like a wide wooden ruler. Aloof, too—at least so far. But then, she had crashed his home.

"My mom and sisters—they signed me up." He leaned against the door frame. For support? His dog could help with that imbalance. Behr had no obvious physical injuries, but then, his wouldn't show that easily. His file read traumatic brain injury. A tough diagnosis, because it wreaked havoc from the inside out. "Didn't mean to make more work for you."

Huh. Interesting. Ellery had never encountered this particular situation before, but then, there was a first time for everything.

"Do you want to come outside? Talk for a

second?" He certainly wasn't inviting her in to discuss things, and it was a gorgeous June day. They'd had a cold May—painful—and the recent boon of warm, seventy-degree weather had felt balmy and therapeutic after a long winter and spring. Even yesterday afternoon's rain had only cooled things down for a few hours.

Behr's vision bobbed to Dash and then landed back on her. "Nope." Steel resolve darkened his eyes to teak.

"Okay." Ellery stretched out the word, not sure where to go from here. "Can I ask why you aren't interested? We're meticulous in matching the right dog to the right injury. We have a remarkably high success rate. These animals change lives." When was the last time she'd had to sell what she did to a veteran? Their waiting list was long. She should just go. Leave him be. But something—maybe a God nudge—had her Keen waterproof boots staying put.

Dash caught sight of a squirrel and took off in its direction, barking and jumping at the base of the tree where it had sought refuge, his nails scraping the bark.

Great. What terrible timing for him to act the complete opposite of the well-trained canine that he was.

You're not selling me or Helping Paws real well here, Dashy-boy.

"That the dog you had picked out for me?" Behr gripped the door frame, his knuckles turning white. Ellery would say he'd inched back, but the movement was so slight she couldn't be sure.

"No. That's my dog. You were matched with a chocolate Lab. Margo."

He gave a curt nod. "I am sorry for the trouble, but I…it's not a fit."

"Dash. Heel." He gave up pursuit and tucked in next to Ellery's left side.

This time there was no mistaking Behr's retreat. He'd removed himself from the screen door by at least half a foot.

"I'm going to put Dash in the truck, and then, would you mind if I came in for a second to talk with you?" She didn't wait for his answer as it was certain to be no. And now that Ellery was possibly clueing in to what was going on, she desperately wanted to get to the bottom of it. She opened the passenger door of her silver Toyota Tacoma, and Dash, assuming they were going for a ride, leaped inside. Little did he know he was getting left out of the next discussion, because Ellery had a theory to test.

She was starting to wonder if instead of seeing a service dog as part of the solution, Behr Delgado saw it as part of the problem.

* * *

Behr Delgado's place was sparse because he didn't own all that much. He had a minimalistic couch and chair, a fifty-inch flat-screen that was disproportionately big for the small living space and a narrow coffee table to prop his feet on. No side tables, because the less furniture he had, the less he bumped into. He kept things as neat as possible—the army had certainly drilled that into him—but since his balance was iffy at best, picking things up and tidying wasn't a simple activity.

While Ellery put her dog in the truck, he quickly collected the few dirty dishes he'd left out and stacked them in the sink. He shoved the pile of bills and mail behind his coffeepot as a temporary fix.

Behr had just gotten home from work and dropped onto the couch, planning to rest for a few minutes when the dog lady had started knocking. While his new occupation at Step Up—a charity that worked to mentor and rehab young men—wasn't anywhere near the physical activity level he'd engaged in while enlisted, it wore him out a thousand times faster. A brain injury had the power to change the whole scope of a person's system. His body had turned foreign, clumsy.

The thing Behr had always been able to count on—his strength—had been ripped from him.

He was learning every day how to work with this new, much less dependable vessel. But he was thankful to be alive. The constant knowledge that numerous friends hadn't made it and had never come home carried its own trauma.

The woman who'd shown up unannounced and then invited herself in reappeared at his screen door. Her hair—the color of ripe Bing cherries—peeked out from under her baseball cap, contrasting with her fair skin. She wore work boots, cuffed olive green pants and a fitted T-shirt that read Eat, Sleep, Dogs. A perfect caption to highlight their differences.

Behr knew the impending conversation was pointless, but he couldn't just refuse her request when she'd obviously put a lot of work into the Service Dog That Was Not To Be.

He waved her inside. "Have a seat. Would you like a glass of water?"

"No, thanks. I won't take up much of your time."

Why did he not believe her? Ellery waited for him to sit—he took the chair since it was easiest for him to get out of—and she perched on the couch cushion like she was paying by the second to rent the space.

"Can I ask you a direct question?"

Behr almost laughed. This woman wore subtlety like a tactical vest. "Go for it."

"I get the impression that my dog—or maybe any dog—is an...*issue* for you."

"That wasn't a question." Her peach lips opened with surprise, and her cheeks popped like they'd been shaded with red crayon. "But your theory is correct. I'm not comfortable around dogs." To say the least. "Too many encounters on my tours with aggressive ones." Behr didn't even like to talk about it, so the idea of getting a dog as a service animal to be with him at all times? No, thank you.

"Can I ask what some of your symptoms are on a daily basis?"

"Lack of balance is the worst of them. But I also experience headaches. Exhaustion. Sensitivity to light and noise. Sometimes blurred vision or dizziness." Though he was extremely careful not to drive if either of those was a possibility, and they usually only happened after extreme fatigue.

Ellery leaned forward in earnest. "Margo would be a huge help for you."

"And how's that going to happen when I can't be around her?" Behr laid it out bluntly because he didn't know how else to get through to her.

"Good question. I'll train you one-on-one." Did she know her hands sliced into the air with every syllable? "Usually I run group classes, but that's obviously not going to work." Obviously. "And it's obviously why you didn't show up today." Obviously. "But I don't want to give up on this without trying. Don't you think it's worth attempting? I could give you contact information of other veterans who've gone through the program. You could ask questions, get some feedback about their experiences. So many of them say their dogs gave them their life back."

No resided on the tip of Behr's tongue. A no that would surely be ignored by this woman. Was she related to his sisters in some form or fashion?

"Other people have tried to acclimate me to dogs. It hasn't worked. It's not like I'm choosing to react this way."

"I'm not saying you are. We don't have to get you to the point that you're okay with all dogs. Just one really, *really* sweet chocolate Lab."

Annoyed amusement climbed his cheeks. "You are nothing if not determined." His four sisters and his mom had gotten it in their heads to sign him up for this program. They'd thought a service dog would be great for him. He'd tried to explain his fear of the animal, but they hadn't listened.

And people said men didn't listen to women.

In his world it was the other way around. He was always getting steamrolled by the females in his family. They'd even pulled out the God card with him. They'd said the waiting list for a service dog was long and that they planned to pray him to the front of it. And if that happened, he was supposed to take it as a sign that God wanted him to do this.

Behr absolutely believed in God and His provision, but he was starting to think his sisters may have done something extra to get him a match this quickly. It should have taken longer. Long enough for him to finagle a way out of this.

"Did my sisters pay you off or something? Because this seems quick."

The fair skin kissing Ellery's eyes crinkled. "No. I would never accept bribes for placements. Believe it or not, I've refused offers like that before."

"You should give her to the next person in line. Someone desperate for her."

"I can't."

"Why? Is there some sort of rule about that? Will she know she's a second choice? Is this like a self-esteem thing? Don't want her to know she was passed by?"

Ellery's laugh was like confetti—light, happy, unburdened. "No. It's just…not only do I work hard to figure out what dog to match to what person, I also pray about it. The nudge is usually God giving me the final seal of approval. And Margo—she was like finding the right puzzle piece, the exact match for your symptoms. I think she'll work well with your issues too." *His issues.* That was a nice way of labeling stark and debilitating fear. "Margo's supersensitive. She's loyal and patient and calm and extremely perceptive to her human's needs. After this conversation, I'm even more convinced she's right for you."

"I can't see how this is going to work. Seems like a waste of your time." *And mine.*

Ellery was leaning so far forward she was practically falling off the couch now. The woman carried enough excitement in her small frame to fill Mile High Stadium.

"All I'm asking is that you try it out. Let's do a few sessions and see how it goes."

"Why?"

"Why try, you mean?"

"Why are you so intent on doing this for me?"

"It's so unusual to not have someone jumping at the chance to get a service dog that I'll admit I was curious as to why." Her arms continued to move quickly, like little exclamation points to her words. "But now that I've met you and I know what's going on, I can't resist wanting to help. It's part of my nature. It's how I ended up running a charity by accident. I started training veteran service dogs as a way to honor my brother, Ace—we lost him in Iraq—and everyone like him who sacrificed so much. But then I got so many applications I couldn't keep up. The need was so great I quit my job to do this full-time. It's not lucrative, but the value goes way beyond money."

How could he say no to her now?

"Fine. We'll do it your way. And after a couple sessions, I'm sure you'll understand why this is a terrible idea."

"Or maybe you'll see all the ways that Margo can assist you and it will change your mind."

Behr wasn't questioning the dog's merit. Just his ability to be around her. His fear of dogs wasn't something he could turn off like a garden hose. And right now, all he could see in his near future was panic and adrenaline and flashbacks.

He certainly hoped Ellery's stubborn resolve paid off. He could use the assistance a service dog would provide, no doubt. But if this experiment didn't work, he was right back to square one—enduring a body that no longer comprehended the messages his injured brain was trying desperately to communicate.

Behr hated to burst Ellery Watson's determined bubble, but he feared she would quickly learn that he was a case that could not be cured.

Chapter Two

"I could use your help scooping in the dog elimination zone." A fancy term for a not-so-fancy job. Was it glamorous work cleaning up after a group of service dogs? No. Was it necessary? Yes. During training weeks, the canines were moved from the volunteer trainers' homes to on-site kennels so the veterans could work with their dog each day. At the end of the week, they'd go home with their new owner.

Her fifteen-year-old nephew scowled in response to her request.

No cowering, Ellery Watson. You're the adult. There's nothing wrong with asking him to help out.

When Fletcher had first arrived, Ellery had attempted to go the "fun aunt" route with him. She'd planned activities for them. Had painstakingly cooked his favorite meals only for him to push food around on his plate. She'd answered his grunts and eye rolls with sweetness and patience.

But she'd quickly learned that bending over backward to please Fletcher didn't work—nothing did.

He was angry about being shipped off to her for the summer. Angry about missing his so-called friends. Angry about…everything. And now she was making him clean up after dogs. How dare she?

"Translation—you want me to scoop poop." Fletcher's black hair spilled past his brows. She'd offered to schedule him an appointment for a haircut with her friend Brynn. He'd—once again—scowled in answer. Apparently *unable to see* was the new style. And apparently thirty-five was the new sixty. Suggesting Fletcher was in need of a haircut sounded like something her parents would say. Not her. But really—how could he see through that curtain?

"That definition works, too." Why sugarcoat it? "And once you're done, please spray the kennels out." Ellery was too tired to mince words with Fletcher. She'd taught another class today for the group of ten veterans who'd received placements. Mt. Vista was located north of Colorado Springs, and most of the veterans had traveled to reach Helping Paws and were staying at hotels or VRBOs for the week of classes. Applicants filled out numerous commitment forms during the paperwork process assuring that they had the funds to feed and provide veterinary care for their dog once the training process was completed, and also committing to the time and travel required for class.

That was why she'd been so irked about Behr not showing up, before she'd understood his reasons. Before she'd found out his mom and sisters had clicked those buttons and made those promises—not him.

"Juvie would be better than this."

"Au contraire, my nephew. Juvenile detention would not be better than cleaning up after dogs."

"Why do you talk that way?"

"'Cause I'm cool."

His eyes rolled. That, he was a professional at.

Fletcher wore jeans, black Vans and a T-shirt that read I Paused My Game to Be Here. His mom had likely paid good money for those shoes.

"Why don't you change first? That way you won't get your clothes or shoes—"

Fletcher took off for the kennel area built off the back of the garage, slamming the door between the two spaces so hard that the building rattled and shook.

"Dirty." Ellery finished. "Thank you for that

exit. This is why you pick your friends wisely!"
Of course he was out of earshot, but she considered continuing the rant in order to pop the balloon of stress his behavior created inside her. Every day more helium was added. Every day the latex stretched. She was running out of space to house the intruder balloon and afraid it was going to pop and take both of them out in the process.

No doubt this was exactly how his mom felt, only amplified.

Desiree had given every ounce of her energy to loving Fletcher. She'd read every parenting book under the sun. She'd gone the sweet route with him. The tough, crack-down route. The supportive-with-boundaries route. Nothing had worked. He was floundering in the ocean without a flotation device.

Ellery didn't understand why he wouldn't just reach out to grab one of their hands.

Instead, Fletcher had jumped in with the wrong crowd in his Denver neighborhood. He was inches from getting arrested, had finished up the school year inches from suspension due to the countless detentions he'd racked up and inches from making his mom yank out every last strand of her espresso hair.

When Desiree had asked Ellery to take Fletcher for part of the summer, hoping the stay in Mt. Vista would bring change for him, they'd wrapped up the two-month visit with a nice bow: *It will be fun! Bonding with your aunt! Working with dogs!* Since Fletcher's dad—Ellery's brother—had died when Fletcher was two, he'd never gotten to know him. Desiree thought living with Ellery could provide part of that missing piece for him. And give her a small break so that she could regroup for the upcoming adolescent years.

But Fletcher, despite making stupid choices, was incredibly smart. He'd read them like the books he refused to touch for school but could fly through if he so desired to. He knew this was a last-ditch effort to reroute his current trajectory, and he was not in the least bit on board. If anything, he was trying to ground the plane before takeoff.

"Hello?" Behr stepped into the training space tentatively—like it was filled with dogs and Ellery was about to unleash them all at once. He could muster up a little more faith in her. She hadn't even removed Margo from her kennel yet. Ellery was planning to go slow, slow, slow, and hoped that maybe, with prayer, this would work.

Behr wore charcoal warm-up pants and a white T-shirt along with running shoes.

So he could escape quickly if need be?

Ever since she'd gone by his place yesterday evening, Ellery had been riddled with doubts about the way she'd convinced—aka forced—him to take part in the program. Who was she to assume she could make this work? War-related trauma regarding dogs was way beyond her scope. And yet, here they were.

"You showed." If she'd learned anything about the man in their short conversation, it was that he had a sense of humor. And Ellery could use some of that in her world. Especially after that encounter with Fletcher.

Training weeks always zapped her energy. Waiting until after the group finished would make sense, but the more time Behr had to think, the more likely he would be to back out completely. Ellery was burning her rope at both ends and praying that the middle would hold.

He chuckled as he approached her. "I appreciate that passive-aggressive greeting."

She smiled and mock bowed. "Thank you."

He glanced around. "Nice place you got here."

"Garage turned training center. It provides what we need for the most part. I'd love to have a space better suited for what we do, but it's hard to use donation money for that versus placing more dogs with more veterans." She didn't have the heart to take money that could save a life and funnel it into office and training space. Maybe someday there would be enough to do both.

"I see you don't have any dogs out."

"I didn't want you to quit before we got started." Ellery motioned toward the house. "Come on. I thought I'd show you a few things first." They walked outside.

Early evening was Ellery's favorite time of day. Usually it meant she was close to being done with work and it was time to figure out dinner. Not that she didn't hop back on her laptop or phone during the evening to tie up loose ends, but the hustle and bustle of office hours, at least, was done.

But since she'd agreed to meet Behr for training after he got off work, her schedule would adjust to that until he was ready to take Margo home...or until they labeled this experiment a failure.

Ellery opened the sliding glass door to the basement, motioning for Behr to enter first. They both wiped their shoes on the mud mat.

Her desk was back to the left. It had a few stacks of paper on it along with her computer, but those were organized according to importance. Ellery kept things tidy since volunteers often worked in the space with her.

There was also a small sitting area by the

fireplace and two volunteer desks that could be used for various projects.

She'd already moved an extra chair behind her desk so she and Behr could both see the screen. She inched her way in first and gave him the easier-to-access seat.

"I thought I'd show you what Margo would be able to do for you first. Might make it more worth the turmoil of adjusting to her if you have a reason to want to." She held up a hand. "I'm not saying the fear is by choice."

"Appreciate that." He settled next to her, smelling like some clean, crisp soap that she definitely appreciated. Most of her veterans came through the program married. Or they were older. But Behr, according to his file, was thirty-four. One year younger than she was. She would imagine he was attached to someone, though he didn't wear a ring and her first impression of his place was definitely bachelor pad.

Ellery opened the clips from one of her previous training sessions. "This is blocking. This could be great for you if you encounter another dog. If we can get you adjusted to Margo, that is. If you're out and another canine approaches, Margo would get in the way, basically. Create a barrier."

Behr listened. Nodded.

She clicked on another video. "And here the dog is assisting someone with a vision impairment…" If or when Behr's vision blurred, Margo would be a huge asset. She started the third video. "She can pick up items around your place and help with anything that would send you off-balance."

"Are you saying my condo was messy? Because you did invite yourself in. Normally people shoot a text or give a little warning before knocking down my door."

She hadn't meant to be offensive by highlighting that Margo could help with picking things up. Sure, there'd been a couple things out at Behr's condo, but he certainly wasn't living at slob levels.

"I didn't mean—"

"Your face—" Behr's eyes sparked with amusement "—is stark white right now."

"You're joking." Of course he was.

"Yep. I do that sometimes."

Or all the time. Ellery was going to have to get better at reading his sense of humor. Either that or spend way too much time apologizing and getting teased for it.

She hit Play on the last video she had queued. "And she'll help you with balance. Most people won't even realize what she's up to, but you should notice a big difference."

"If I can stand to be around her."

"Right." A second stress balloon filled with a puff of helium snuggled inside her next to Fletcher's. "I was thinking that first I'd crate her in the training area so you can be near her but still have separation. That way you can get used to her mannerisms. Learn a bit about her temperament." She stood. "Let's walk out back."

"Do we have to?"

Behr fell into step beside her as they exited the basement door. Once inside the training building, she left him to go leash up Margo. She'd already moved a crate into the training space, so she returned and crated her.

Ellery tugged two chairs over to the crate. Not so close that Behr would want to escape immediately, but enough that he could get a glimpse of who Margo was.

She dropped into one. Behr stood ten feet back, considering.

"You can stay there. It's up to you. I just wanted you to meet her." Her phone rang. It was one of the businesses considering making Helping Paws their charity for the year. "Do you feel okay if I answer this real quick?" She held up her cell.

At the affirmative from Behr, she swiped to answer, then stood and walked outside to give herself some privacy.

When the door swung shut, Behr was rooted in the same spot, leaving her wondering what her next step was if this introduction didn't work…and not wanting to admit to anyone that she didn't have a plan B.

Behr was a burden. A fifty-thousand-pound weight on a bridge that was only built to support half of that. What was wrong with him that man's best friend was his greatest enemy? But then, most people hadn't had experiences like his with vicious stray dogs while deployed. They only saw the sweet, family-pet sides of the animal.

Behr grabbed the chair that Ellery had placed close to the crate and hauled it back a handful of steps. Obviously Margo couldn't get out right now, so he had nothing to fear. And even if she were to get out, logic told him that she was more likely to lick his hand than attack him. But sometimes logic just didn't compute in his rattled brain.

"So. You're my match, huh?" Margo's chin rested on her paws, and at the sound of his voice, she popped up, tail wagging so fast she could churn butter with it. She nosed around the crate on his side. "I think you should go to someone else. You and me, we don't really make sense together."

She plunked down onto the base of the crate like he'd broken off an engagement the week before the wedding.

"That seems a little dramatic."

A faint whine answered him.

Ellery was still on the phone, causing Behr to quadruple-guess this plan yet again. She didn't have time to be doing this for him.

When he'd walked into the garage converted to training space, the entrance had housed a number of informational flyers. Dates for various trainings. Ways to give and volunteer. Websites with additional resources.

The woman must never sleep.

She'd been right to show him the videos first. All of those things would be helpful to him. He'd noticed a sign on the office wall about the emotional support each dog gave to their owner in addition to physical help. But that was the thing that worried him the most. He already struggled with flashbacks to the aggressive dogs he'd encountered during his tours. Sure, there'd been the occasional military K-9, but Behr had steered clear of those enough that he doubted anyone had caught on to his aversion to the animal.

Maybe he should have been more vocal, and he wouldn't have ended up here. But then, he'd admitted the truth to his sisters and mom, and they sure hadn't listened.

"Sorry about that." Ellery strode back into the room. She wore the same ankle work boots from yesterday along with jeans and a navy V-neck, the short sleeves rolled over biceps that shouted, *We may be small but don't underestimate us.* She had on makeup—not too dark or overdone—and her shoulder-length hair was loosely curled—aka beachy—a style he'd heard far too much about because: sisters. Her only jewelry was a simple silver ring with a cross on her right hand.

Ellery had to be around five-five or five-six, but she held herself like she was seven feet tall. Confident. Definitely the type of strong, capable woman Behr appreciated and respected, because again: sisters.

She'd certainly wrangled him over here when he'd had no intentions of agreeing to this.

"How are you feeling right now? Doing okay? Do you want me to take her back to her kennel?"

"No. She's fine."

"Okay, good." She moved her chair closer to his and lifted her hand to let Margo get some licks through the crate's open metal squares. "I meant to ask you—do you have a significant other?"

Was she fishing to see if he was in a relationship? That seemed strange. "Yes, I'm…attached to someone." Behr wasn't in a romantic relationship, but Ellery didn't need to know that, because for all intents and purposes, he was taken. His best friend and platoon-mate had died during their last tour, and Behr had come home injured but determined to support his friend's wife and two kids—who were now four and six years old. As far as relationships were concerned, Marina and those children were his sole focus. There wasn't room in his life for anyone else.

"Oh, I didn't—" Ellery sighed. "I didn't mean for it to come out like that. I'm sorry. I wasn't digging to see if you were in a relationship. I meant—it was about making sure you had a support system and people watching out for you. Because the training goes much better when you do." She ran agitated fingers through her burgundy hair. "I'm sorry, Behr. I just had a thing…a conversation with my nephew before you arrived, and it rattled me. I'm not articulating very well."

"It's okay." Getting his relationship on the table wasn't a terrible idea anyway. He and Ellery had to be close in age. And she was… intriguing. The combination of her fair skin, her colorful hair, those green eyes that sparked with flecks of yellow. Nothing wrong with her knowing he was committed to someone. Not that she'd given him any impression she was interested in him but still…didn't hurt to lay things out.

"I've started off on the wrong foot with you twice now."

"Guess that's why God gave us two feet." She was hard on herself. Behr had that same tendency. But Ellery hadn't done anything offensive. At least, not in his opinion. Everything she did seemed to come from a good place. A helpful place. "I also have my family around. My parents and one sister live in Mt. Vista and are always available to help me. My other three sisters are spread out over the Front Range, but if I needed any of them, they'd show up in an instant."

Behr let that realization settle like Alka-Seltzer fizzing to the bottom of a glass. He had it pretty good. Despite his annoyance at his family for butting in by signing him up for a service dog, he knew their meddling came from a place of love.

Ellery's face had morphed at his admission. A flash of pain registered. Then a pop of envy. And then acceptance.

It seemed impossible that Behr could glean all of that from her expression. And yet…it had been right there. He got the impression that the question she'd just asked of him had a completely different answer when it came to her. Which begged him to ask…who supported Ellery Watson while she supported everyone else?

"That…that's perfect. Good. I'm so glad you have all those options." Ellery blinked to clear emotion that had bubbled to the surface following Behr's answer. The encounter with Fletcher must have messed with her more than she'd realized. She'd never imagined a simple *do you have support* question would implode so quickly.

She was embarrassed that Behr had thought she was snooping. And not the least bit surprised that he was in a relationship. But the family support…that had gutted her before she'd even had time to hold up a defensive hand.

Ellery's world didn't resemble Behr's. She had people, but not at the same level. She had Brynn, who'd started out as her hairstylist and quickly turned into her closest friend. She was the mastermind behind Ellery's current deep auburn locks. And Ellery's parents were somewhat supportive from afar because they gave money to Helping Paws regularly, but they only visited her about once a year and their communication with her was sporadic. She often wondered if it was painful for them to be around her after

Ace's death and if that's why they didn't have a closer relationship. And her sister-in-law needed support more than she could give it right now, which was understandable.

But all of that left Ellery feeling adrift at times. Especially since Ace had been her closest friend. That rundown from Behr had made Ellery miss him with such an acute ache it was as if he'd passed away this morning.

It was hard to lose your person. To recall anew every morning that they were gone, to start typing a text to them a decade after the fact only to remember they didn't have that communication option in heaven.

"I feel like I owe you a similar explanation, since I accidentally forced you to spill. I'm in a relationship, too. With this charity." Pathetic? Sure. Honest? Definitely. "I eat, sleep, dream and obsess Helping Paws. Sounds unhealthy, I suppose, but it's just where I'm at right now. We're about to get some consistent support, and I hope to take things to the next level with it. I have a laundry list of items to improve." Crude words sounded through the back door to the kennels, and a round of barking followed. Behr tensed. Ellery motioned in that direction. "And now I have my teenage nephew, Fletcher, to concentrate on. My brother, Ace, who passed away—his son. Dealing with Fletcher is like running four charities, God bless him. And if you repeat that, I'll deny it."

Behr's chuckle was on the quiet side. Low and easy and smooth. It upped her comfort level with him yet another notch.

"You know, if both of us weren't otherwise attached, that episode with you knocking down my door yesterday would've been our meet-cute."

What was he talking about? "I'm sorry, what?"

"A meet-cute. Like in *You've Got Mail*. Or *The Holiday*."

"I have no idea what you're saying right now."

"You don't know what a meet-cute is?"

"From movies? Or books? Sure. I know what that is. But I don't know why you're talking about it."

"I was just saying that if we weren't both taken, yesterday would have been ours." He hunched his shoulders, mimicked someone pounding fists. "Hey! Let me in! You didn't show up for your dog and I'm mad!" His fal-setto voice had Ellery clamping her lips shut to keep a smile from sprouting.

"That's a terrible impression of me. And I didn't *knock down* your door."

"Maybe not physically, but mentally you were totally there. Admit it—you had an Incredible

Hulk moment. You were pretty peeved that I hadn't shown up for the first training. At least until you figured out why."

How did he nail her like that? She had been upset. She'd felt her time had been disrespected.

"How do you know what a meet-cute is? Are you sure you were in the army?"

"I have four sisters. I know all things female. How do you think I got signed up for a dog I'm afraid of?"

Ellery laughed. It was a good thing that they were both "taken" as he'd put it. Behr could be a big distraction if she let him be. But she didn't have time for that. The phone call she'd just finished had been very promising. A local company planned to donate consistently during their next fiscal year, starting in July. Helping Paws' first corporate sponsor. It was the kind of money that could really change things. Ellery refused to avert her concentration from assisting veterans in order to focus on a distraction who'd just assured her he wasn't even that.

But she could admit Behr was quickly turning into more than just an acquaintance. Either he was different than the other veterans who had come through the program—more personable or *something* she couldn't put her finger on—or he just felt different because she'd never done one-on-one sessions in the past. And she'd definitely never *knocked down* a veteran's door before to uncover why they hadn't showed for class.

Ellery wouldn't be surprised in the least to find out that Behr had caught on to her emotional distress a minute ago and started that whole meet-cute bit just to get her laughing.

If so, it had worked. And so had distracting him.

During their conversation, Behr had inched closer to her, and in turn, closer to Margo. Even if the step was small, he was in the same room with a dog he was no longer thinking about. That had to be a small victory, didn't it?

Should she try opening the crate and letting Margo out while leashed?

A crash sounded and the door leading to the kennels slammed open.

"I'm not doing this anymore!" Fletcher's shout was loud enough to be heard a mile away, his anger molten enough to set the building on fire.

So much for the small victory of Behr getting comfortable in Margo's presence, because Ellery was headed right back into battle. And she was quickly losing hope of gaining any ground in the war to reroute Fletcher. A disappointment, because she didn't want to lose any more of the family she had left.

Especially not Ace's son, when he would give anything to be here himself.

Chapter Three

The nephew that Ellery had mentioned now appeared in human form. He stomped into the training room like a villain in a Marvel movie—arms flailing with anger, his pale skin splotchy. Behr wouldn't be surprised if he hit a button and started flying around and destroying things.

"I stepped in a pile of—"

"We get the idea," Ellery interrupted.

"And then when I was spraying out the kennels, *stuff* got all over me." He noticed Behr and stopped in his tracks. Hesitation surfaced, as if he knew better than to continue in front of a veteran. As if his aunt would be mortified by his behavior. But then he clicked back into angry teenager mode, refocusing his red-hot fury on Ellery. "This is manual labor! I don't even think it's legal. You shouldn't be allowed to make me work like this without paying me."

The kid should try out basic training.

"I'm happy to pay you, Fletcher."

Why pay him? If he was living here, he should be required to help out. Especially since Ellery was running a charity, not some Fortune 500 company.

"All you've done since I got here is tell me what to do and make me work. I should call child protective services and report you."

Ellery's back went ramrod straight, and her mouth formed the same *O* it had when she'd dropped by Behr's condo yesterday. Fletcher had landed a direct hit with that one. Behr had half a mind to intervene with this punk, but it really wasn't his place.

"You're only saying you'll pay me 'cause there's a witness." His chin jutted in Behr's direction.

This teenager was excellent at being…teenager-y.

What did he get out of an outburst like this? Attention? Assurance that he was loved?

Behr barely knew Ellery, but he was confident she was giving the kid both of those things and more. He only had to look at what she did for veterans she didn't even know to confirm that.

"Fletcher. Please stop. I have someone here. We can talk about this later." Ellery's tone was smooth sailing, but the tendons in her wrist and neck were strung tight like guitar strings.

"Whatever. We won't talk about it later. You don't have time for that. You're always on your laptop or phone."

"Working!" Heat sizzled in Ellery's response. "I've put my laptop away at eight every night since you got here. I'm willing to hang out, but you're always hiding in your room. When I ask you to be part of making dinner, you grunt and disappear. I'm trying here, Fletch. I promise I'm trying. And I'm on my phone and computer because I'm helping people. You should try it sometime."

Behr resisted a whistle and a standing ovation.

"I'm out of here." Fletcher stalked toward the exit.

"Where are you going?"

The door slammed. Ellery's hands twisted like a dryer full of towels, and those yellow flecks in her green eyes were highlighted with moisture.

"I'm so sorry about that. That was *completely* unprofessional. Between you thinking I was asking if you were in a relationship and that, I wouldn't be surprised if you never came back after today."

Of course Ellery would care about how things

looked, how they ran. But Behr understood that life and people never went according to plan. He certainly hadn't penciled in shrapnel imbedding into his skull.

"I'm not a whole class of veterans about to leave a negative Google review, Ellery. I have a misfiring brain. Sometimes my balance is as good as a one-year-old learning to walk, and I was a teenage boy once, too. But I had my dad. I get it. It's okay to be real with me."

"Thank you." Her smile wobbled with emotion, and her exhale was shaky.

"I think we're going to have to reclassify this." He motioned between them. "So that you can stop apologizing every time something isn't 'professional.'" He used air quotes.

"Acquaintances?"

"Nah. We've gone beyond that."

"Certainly after that episode we just did."

"Probably have to call it a friendship. That's the only description that fits. Or at least what's going to fit after we spend more time together. And since that's in our plans…it only makes sense."

"So we'll just…fast-forward to it." Her lips morphed from a straight line of tension to a curve of acceptance. "Since that's where we'll end up eventually anyway."

He grinned. "Exactly." Ever since Fletcher

had stormed into the training room, an idea had been growing for Behr. An idea that maybe he could help her out with one thing that would lighten her load.

It was the least he could do since she was attempting to lighten his.

"In the interest of being *friends*," Ellery continued, "I'd like to say, I really wish I hadn't tacked on that last bit to Fletcher. That was overkill. He just…oh, he pushes my buttons, but it's not an excuse. I'm the adult. I shouldn't lose it like that."

"He's a teenager. His whole job is button pushing. It's like he's at an airplane console with toddler trigger fingers."

She laughed, and that lead weight he'd resembled earlier lightened by a couple thousand pounds.

"You didn't say anything terrible. You were right. If he helped other people, he might stop focusing on his own troubles." It was part of what Step Up believed. They always had the boys who attended MENtor camp participate in community service.

"Still, I'm sorry for what I said. And for what all he said. He's just—"

"A teenager? Angry at the world? Bitter about losing his dad? None of that's on you, Ellery."

Those barely-there tears from a minute ago

resurfaced and threatened to spill. Behr recognized that look because: sisters. His household while he was growing up had been a revolving door of hormones, tears, boy discussions and fighting over clothes. Plus lots of chick flicks and rom-coms. He and Dad had always been outnumbered. It had bonded them, especially since Dad had been in the army his whole career.

"I understand the pressure you feel to help him." Behr's family would absolutely assist each other if they were to encounter a similar situation. "To save him." Because ultimately, wasn't that what she was trying to do? But Behr wasn't sure that was humanly possible. Based on what he'd witnessed, some divine intervention might be in order.

"I was so naive. When my sister-in-law asked me to keep him for part of the summer, I didn't realize it would be this hard. That he'd become so...jaded. Lost. I should not have said yes. He hates it here."

"I'm going to go out on a limb and say the Fletcher I just saw would hate it anywhere right now."

The worry lines that had sprouted on her face softened. Faded. "Yeah. True."

"You're keeping him alive. My..." Friend? Significant other? How should he label Marina? "She has two little ones, and her motto is *keep 'em alive*. Feed them, bathe them. Survive. Those years are hard. Teenage years are hard in a different way."

"That has to be a lot of work for her. I'm glad they have you." If only he made up for what they'd lost.

Ellery continued, "Fletcher does have good moments. Sometimes he forgets to be snarly, and he'll tell me something funny about his mom. Or a story about them visiting my parents in Montana. I often wonder if he should have gone there for the summer, but I'm not sure my parents could handle him anyway. He's…a lot."

"He's extra, for sure."

"My parents never really recovered from losing my brother. Haven't been themselves ever since."

"Have you?"

"Not fully, I suppose. But I'm doing my best."

"Any other siblings?"

"No. Just us." Which made Ellery an only child now.

In Behr's opinion, you never fully recovered from loss. You morphed into the next version of yourself. The version with a gunshot wound right through the heart. It pumped but never in quite the same way.

A gush of air whooshed out of Ellery. "Wow. Feel like I've been to therapy today."

"Better you than me." He'd done his share of physical therapy and some of the other stuff, too.

Her mouth echoed the arc of his. "I guess this is why I don't usually do private training. I become an actual human then."

"You don't do private training sessions because you don't have the time. You have a lot going on. I saw those signs by the door. All those trainings you're doing. I shouldn't be taking up your time like this. Especially since it may not even work." Behr couldn't envision it working, but he didn't want to push Ellery under when she was already barreling downstream.

"You're not backing out that fast! You said you'd give me a few sessions."

"I'm not backing out. I'm just saying you're running a charity on your own. That has to be exhausting."

"You're dealing with brain trauma on the daily. That has to be exhausting, too. We all have our thing."

True. And between the two of them, they seemed to have ten "things" total. Despite the fact that Ellery was helping him out, Behr got the distinct impression that this next conversation he was going to bring up would be quite the fight.

* * *

Behr motioned to the crate. "My pulse has calmed down now that Margo is sleeping." Amusement softened his features, erasing some of the anxiety that had been evident when he'd walked into the training room.

While the minuscule progress of today might not be a lot for anyone else, Ellery was counting it as a victory. The Behr balloon inside her released a smidgen of helium. Margo was a calm dog—part of why Ellery felt she'd be a good fit for Behr. That, and she was incredibly sensitive to her trainer's emotions. Being crated instead of out comforting Behr or Ellery had probably exhausted her to the point that she'd given up on assisting them like she'd wanted to and given in to sleep.

"Listen, I have an idea." Behr edged closer, earnest. "I work at Step Up. We host MENtor camps for young men. We teach them what to look for in friends, how to recognize and stand up to the wrong kind of influence. We teach them to dream about a future and give them ways to reach it by offering follow-up programs. I wonder if it could be a good fit for Fletcher and where he's at."

She'd expected him to have an idea about training with Margo, not a suggestion for Fletcher. But all those things he'd listed would be amazing for her nephew. "I mean…that sounds like something he could use. His neighborhood has some tough kids in it, and he fell in with them. That's why Desiree wanted to get him out of there for the summer." His neighborhood also had good kids, according to Desiree. She didn't understand what made Fletcher flock to the troubled ones instead of the ones with potential. Her sister-in-law blamed herself, but Ellery kept assuring her that she'd done her best, was still doing her best. There wasn't a more loving mother this side of the Continental Divide. She gave every bit of time and energy she had to her son. She prayed over him endlessly. Sometimes everything just wasn't enough.

"We have a summer MENtor camp starting next week that goes for two weeks. Being that Fletcher is local and wouldn't need to stay onsite, I imagine I could squeeze him in. If you're interested, I can talk to my superior."

Should Ellery feel this much relief over Behr's offer? Was this what Desiree had felt in orchestrating this summer break? No. Sending Fletcher to live with Ellery had been a sacrifice, not a relief. And yet she'd done it because she believed the change would help. That a smaller town would help. That maybe getting to know his dad from Ellery's perspective would help.

"I don't want to put you in the position of

asking for special treatment for him." Ellery imagined Step Up had a waiting list just like Helping Paws did.

"You mean like what you're doing for me here?"

"That's different."

"Is it?"

He'd stumped her. She was veering out of the boundaries to help him individually. She was squeezing extra work hours into her day to assist him.

"I don't need anything from you in return for Margo training. That's not how it works."

"And yet, one-on-one sessions isn't how it works, either. I'm not accepting your help if you're not going to accept mine."

Well, well, well. He'd backed her into a corner. And truly, it was a corner she wanted to be shoved into. Ellery felt weak needing help with Fletcher when he was only here for six weeks. Shouldn't she be able to do this? Was she working too much, like Fletcher had said? Was that why he was acting out?

If her nephew had come with a manual, that would have been nice.

How could Ellery just pass off the duty of mentoring Fletcher onto Step Up? Wasn't that cheating?

"I'll talk to his mom and get her thoughts

on it. If she thinks it would be good, then I'm game. I just don't want her thinking that I'm ditching time with him or too overwhelmed to handle him."

"Talking to her is a great idea, since we'll need her to sign him up. And I'm not saying either of you are too overwhelmed to handle him. I'm just saying it's okay to have assistance. I've seen the program work since I started there, and I've heard plenty of testimonials from before my employment." Behr's head tilted along with one corner of his mouth. "Kind of like you've convinced me that Helping Paws works."

She had convinced him of that. And Ellery imagined that Step Up's strategy for reaching Fletcher would be far more developed and successful than hers.

"I'm not used to being the one taking." She hadn't realized that being in the position of giving was easier until right at this moment. That was why she received so many notes and emails of encouragement and thanks from her veterans. It was a humbling thing to receive instead of give.

"Tough on the other side, isn't it, kid?" He grinned as if knowing he had her. "Now you know how I feel. Losing my strength and agility after this injury was devastating. When you've always been the person who handles things, not being able to handle anything is, well…awful."

"That makes a whole lot of sense." The more Ellery got to know Behr, the more she liked him, the more she was glad she'd pushed him into trying this experiment. If Margo could help him, it would all be worth it. "I'll call Desiree tonight, providing I don't have to drive around town searching for Fletcher."

"He'll show up when he's hungry. It's the number one emotion boys have."

"That's not an emotion."

"It is, to boys."

She laughed. Ellery had a feeling she was going to be doing a lot of that in the next few weeks and that maybe it was just what she needed. Behr thought she was helping him, but based on their current conversation and the humor he brought into her world, it just might turn out to be the other way round.

Chapter Four

I cannot believe you bought Jakey a Jeep!

The text from Marina popped onto Behr's phone as he was waiting for Fletcher to get dropped off at Step Up. Though MENtor camp started next week, Behr was taking the opportunity to introduce Fletcher to the Step Up ranch today. He planned to give him a tour of the grounds, a quick rundown of the ins and outs of what MENtor camp entailed and do something fun with him. That last part should really throw the teen off.

Behr was expecting an angry, petulant Fletcher to show up—if he showed at all.

After his disappearing act the other night, Ellery had texted Behr to let him know that he'd been right. Fletcher had reappeared two hours after he'd stomped out of the training room—grumpy, hungry and in one piece. Thank God.

Unsurprisingly, Fletcher's mom, Desiree, had given a big, resounding *yes, please* to him taking part in MENtor camp. She'd filled out the paperwork in record time, and Behr had slid him into a last-minute spot after convincing his supervisor that Fletcher's need was strong, and his current proximity provided a rare opportunity.

He may have also relayed that Fletcher had lost his father during the Iraq war.

Behr wasn't ashamed to play the war hero card with Jasper, who had great respect for any vet. How else would Behr have gotten a job at a place like Step Up? He hadn't exactly been qualified for a position at the charity. But Jasper had taken Behr in and trained him in numerous areas. Scheduling, answering parent emails, working with other staffers on special events, handling logistics for the campers who were bussed or flown in for the program.

Behr had even begun leading the small group breakout sessions that focused on military careers. They showcased all kinds of occupations in order to get the boys dreaming and envisioning their futures. And while Behr wasn't a trained mentor and didn't stay on-site for MENtor camp, Jasper had asked Behr to take on that role casually with Fletcher. Basically, introduce him to the place, be his contact. Watch out for the kid. Have him come by today to show him there was more than just work involved in MENtor camp and maybe gain an inch of his trust.

Both he and Jasper believed Fletcher was going to be a tough nut to crack.

Step Up's offices were at the entrance to the property, the activity buildings further west. Behr scanned the parking lot from his office window. No sign of Fletcher as of yet. He'd offered to pick up the teen for the afternoon knowing that Ellery had a group training session today, but she'd replied that her friend Brynn would drop him off after lunch.

Behr settled into his chair and took the opportunity to respond to Marina. My job is to spoil them.

This is beyond spoiling!

A photo popped up of little Jakey in the driver's seat of the black, lifted child-sized Jeep Behr had sent for his sixth birthday. He was headed to first grade in a few short months, which somehow felt so much bigger and older than kindergarten. Jakey wore sunglasses, sported a grin missing a tooth, and was giving a thumbs-up.

He looks like he was meant for that thing.

There was a moment after it arrived that I considered sending it back. The box showed what it was, and Jakey hadn't seen it yet. It just seems like too much, B.

Too much? The kids' dad—Marina's husband—was gone forever. A toy Jeep paled in comparison to that kind of loss.

If it distracts them, keeps them happy or just gives any of you a good day, it's worth it.

Another picture came through of little Adira, who was four, riding in the passenger seat. The pure delight on her face tempted him to send another one in pink. But that would be overkill. See? He was controlled.

Marina and the kids lived in Louisiana. He asked how things were going otherwise, and she said it was already blazing hot and the kids were in swimming lessons at the community pool.

You're doing a great job with them! Can't wait to see you guys in a few weeks.

When their schedules could swing it, Behr popped down to visit for a long weekend, and he'd recently booked the next one. Jakey and Adira referred to him as Uncle Behr, which they thought was funny because they were no doubt thinking *bear*. They often requested that he growl and chase after them, and Behr happily agreed. It was the kind of thing Jake would have done.

Behr knew he'd never replace the kids' father, and he wasn't trying to. He just considered it his job to support all three of them. Jake would have done the same if their roles had been reversed. While so many of Behr's fellow soldiers had become part of his extended family, Jake had become his brother. They'd bonded over their faith, their values, their similar senses of humor. Behr had lost the best friend he'd ever known when he'd lost Jake.

Caring for Marina and the kids was his way of triaging that wound.

When his sisters had learned about his close relationship with Marina, they'd instantly jumped to the conclusion that it was romantic. It had taken Behr a while to convince them it was not. While he respected and cared for Marina very much, there wasn't a spark between them. Romance had never been on the table.

The phone on Behr's desk beeped, and the

older gentleman who worked the front reception desk spoke.

"Behr, you have a young man named Fletcher here to see you."

"On my way." He let out an extended exhale as he strode to the front lobby. This should be interesting.

He'd told Fletcher to dress casually, perhaps for an outdoor activity. Fletcher hadn't responded to his text, but he was wearing gym shorts, old-school high-tops, and a Led Zeppelin T-shirt that hung on his lanky frame. Fletcher registered an inch or two below Behr's height of five foot ten, though he wouldn't be surprised to find the teen passing him soon.

"Hey, man. Come on back to my office." Behr led the way, and Fletcher shuffled behind. When they reached the small office, Behr motioned for him to take a seat in one of the two chairs facing his desk.

Fletcher's descent was as dramatic as Lebron after a supposed foul.

Some boys wanted to attend MENtor camp. Others were being forced.

Fletcher obviously fell into the second category. But if they could reach him now—before he got arrested, before he abused more substances than the cigarettes his Mom had mentioned—it would be a huge victory.

It was killing Behr not to know what had convinced him to come.

"I'm only here because my mom and Aunt Ellery promised me a dog of my own if I do your stupid program."

That explained so much. Well done to Ellery and Desiree. A dog would be really great for Fletcher, who obviously wasn't traumatized by them like Behr, and using one as a reward was smart. It would undoubtedly create more expense and work for his mom, but she was willing to pay that price for Fletcher to gain this experience. Based on Behr's interactions with her so far, he wasn't surprised by her sacrifice.

"Works for me."

Fletcher glanced around the office. "So, what now? Do I have to watch a video or something? Go to class?"

During MENtor camp, they had daily sessions, motivational speakers, sports, outstanding food, lots of fun and breakout sessions with their mentor.

The boys who came from out of the area stayed at the ranch for the duration of the two-week program. But Step Up was able to add an additional twenty-five boys by allowing day campers who lived in the vicinity of the program. Fletcher wouldn't be the only one coming and going each day, but he was most definitely the last to slide into a spot.

Behr had witnessed great changes from weekend mentoring sessions throughout the spring. He was excited to see how much more would come from a two-week session. Since this would be his first summer experience, he and Fletcher would both be newbies.

"Next week there will be some classes, but today I'm going to give you a tour. Show you what to expect from camp. And we get to do something fun. One of Step Up's activities. You're in charge of choosing what we do."

If Behr hadn't been watching closely, he would have missed the spark of interest that flashed like distant lightning across the teen's features.

"Whatever."

Behr stemmed his amusement at Fletcher's unsurprising response. "Exactly. Whatever we want. Here's a list of things available to us." He slipped the brochure across the desk, and Fletcher slowly picked it up like it was a rattlesnake. Like touching it was the equivalent to sticking a fork in an electrical outlet. Like his terrible-influence friends were watching through the windows and about to pound him for making a choice that wasn't ill-advised.

Fletcher scanned through the options, which

were tempting because they'd been designed to be. Horseback riding. Four-wheeling. Zip-lining. Step Up had numerous activities that would capture the young men's interest…despite how much they didn't want to let on that they had any.

He slapped the brochure back onto the desk. "Don't care."

"Okay. I'll choose, then." Which one would Fletcher hate the most? Behr went with his gut. "Let's zip-line."

The kid's nose wrinkled.

Perfect. Behr had found something he didn't care to do…which meant there was something on that list that intrigued him.

"I don't get it," Fletcher said gruffly as he studied the floor, his shoes, the dime-sized hole at the bottom of his T-shirt. "What's the catch?"

"No catch. There's no lesson in it." Except to show Fletcher he had value and worth. Behr nodded to the brochure. "Do you want to take another look?"

"Are you doing this with me?"

"Yep. Just you and me today."

"Isn't your head too messed up for some of this?"

"No more than your lungs are from how much you've been smoking—according to your mom's intel."

When Behr had spoken to Desiree, she'd been emotionally grateful about the program, weeping on the other end of the phone, thanking him for doing this. Behr had assured her none of this was because of him. Step Up had existed before him, and if he ever changed careers, they'd exist after him.

Helping Fletcher was only fitting because of what Ellery was doing for him. And even more than that, it was just the right thing to do when a drowning kid was within reach, and Behr could yank him out of a river that would eventually overtake him.

"Shouldn't you be nicer to me?" Fletcher's arms crossed and he plopped against the back of his chair, his body language two syllables from sliding right out of the seat.

Behr shrugged. "Probably. If you're asking if any of those are off-limits for me, the answer is no." Behr was as much of an adventurist as the next guy. He wasn't going to let TBI keep him from doing fun stuff for the rest of his life.

So many soldiers with traumatic brain injuries were worse off than he was. Some couldn't wash their car in the driveway without the activity demolishing them. Some had major processing issues. Short- or long-term memory lapses. Some couldn't work at all.

Behr's family had been so on top of his care

when he'd first been injured that they'd finagled the right kind of help right away. He was certain that was why he could function as well as he did.

It was no wonder they'd signed him up for a service dog. After their initial success with pushing the doctors and medical staff and demanding exceptional care for him, they thought they were invincible.

Behr was grateful and annoyed with them on the daily.

Fletcher didn't pick up the brochure again, but he did answer. "Fine. Four-wheeling."

"Let me call down to reserve a couple and then we'll get going. I wonder if you should have pants, though, in case you spill."

"One, I'm not planning to spill, and two, if you can do it with a messed-up head, I'll be fine without pants."

Behr chuckled, not sure what either of those things had to do with each other, but as Fletcher would say, whatever.

He made a call and they drove one of the golf carts out to the activities center where the equipment was kept. Step Up had quite a bit of land. The zip-line, horses and four-wheelers were all on-site. They were definitely bringing in more money than Helping Paws. Behr would feel worse about that, but he wasn't the one in charge of donations. He'd pray that God would provide what Helping Paws needed. Ellery was certainly doing her part to make that happen. And Behr could only hope he would be able to do his part to reach the sullen, quiet teen riding next to him.

After a long day of training—and one veteran who'd played twenty questions about his new service dog—the training center had finally emptied.

But before Ellery could so much as take a swig from her water bottle, she'd gained a new guest. One of her older veterans who'd been through the training program years before showed up to tell her his dog had passed away.

He'd hoped that she might have another one on hand for him. Somehow Ellery had managed not to snort or cackle at his request. If only training service dogs was so easy that she could have a few on reserve for situations like this.

She sat next to Nico on the bench that lined the wall, patting his back like he was six months old instead of seventy-plus.

"Herman saved my life. I can't go anywhere without him, but with him, I felt human again."

The beauty of the service dog in a nutshell. Ellery felt his anguish with every bone in her body. The pressure to fix this was suffocating…

and he was just one of the many veterans on her list. All she wanted to do was help. All she could do was follow the steps she did for everyone else. Ellery couldn't multiply herself or the resources. Not without more money and people and trained dogs. That was what Nico didn't understand. He wasn't the only one desperate, and Ellery simply didn't have the means to get everyone a dog as fast as requested or needed.

"Nico, we will find you another dog. It might take a little time, but we will. I need you to hang on for a little bit, okay?"

He swiped tears from his face and nodded.

"Did you drive yourself here?" Ellery hoped not. She wasn't sure how he'd make it home to Pueblo if he had.

"No. My daughter drove me."

"She could have come in."

"She was embarrassed of me."

"I doubt that's true if she drove you here."

"Not of the PTSD. She's seen the likes of that firsthand. She wanted me to call instead of showing up like this."

Smart daughter. "That would have been good. You can do that next time you need to talk to me, okay?" Ellery squeezed his arm. "I hear you. I see you. And I'm so sorry about Herman. I'm going to send the online application link to your email."

"But I already—"

"I know you already had a dog, and I know it's frustrating that I'm asking you to do the application again, but your needs may have changed since you were matched the first time." Plus, if Nico filled everything out, then a volunteer could assist with matching him. Otherwise, it was all on Ellery and her memories of what Nico's biggest issues were. And while Ellery recalled most if not all of the veterans who had filed through Helping Paws, she didn't have a computer for a brain. "Fill it out for me, okay? Have your daughter help."

A noise from near the entrance notified Ellery she had more visitors. Hopefully, it wasn't another emergency, because she was spent. Behr stood just inside the door to the training room.

Oh-no-oh-no-oh-no. She'd forgotten to pick up Fletcher. Nico had distracted her after training, and she'd totally spaced on her nephew.

What a worm-infested cherry on top of this moment.

When Nico struggled to push up from the bench, Behr wordlessly joined them, supporting him. They walked on each side of Nico as he shuffled to the door. A bit like they were sending him off to prison instead of home with his daughter.

They reached the car and Behr opened the passenger door.

"I'm so sorry," the woman behind the steering wheel, who looked to be midforties, apologized. "I tried to convince him this was a terrible idea."

"It's okay." It wasn't, and yet, what was Ellery going to say? She couldn't crush Nico any more than he already was.

They got Nico seated and his daughter backed out of the drive, giving an apologetic wave before accelerating.

"You need to move the training center offsite."

"This is why we should have an actual training center instead of running things from my home."

Behr and Ellery spoke at the same time. The first smile in an hour tugged on her mouth.

There was definitely no privacy with training happening on her property, but the work had to be done. Nico was a prime example of that.

"You get visitors dropping by like that a lot?"

"No. Everyone is respectful, but Nico…he's just broken. I can't blame him for showing up."

"I can." Behr was on high alert, his stance protective, scanning her driveway as if someone else was going to roll in. At which time he would escort them off her property like a bouncer. Like a knight. Like a really good, supportive friend. Ellery softened. Well. That was a nice balm to the painful scratch Nico's visit had just imparted.

"He was hoping that I'd have a dog lazing around, fully trained, that he could take home." A third helium balloon materialized, and Ellery envisioned chopping it in half like that Fruit Ninja game she sometimes played on her phone to decompress. She didn't have room inside of her for another balloon.

"He knows that's not how it works," she continued, "but he doesn't know how to live without Herman."

"Ellery." Behr's voice dropped low and far too gentle. She knew what was coming next. "Why don't you—"

"Nope." Behr was going to offer up Margo, but that wouldn't solve anything. Behr needed assistance, too. Everyone was important. Nico's anguish didn't diminish Behr's hardships. "I take it you brought my nephew home when I forgot to pick him up."

Behr paused, slowly accepting her change of subject. "I was driving back anyway. And I wouldn't say you forgot him as much as you were unexpectedly delayed."

"That definitely sounds better. How'd it go

with Fletcher?" Ellery glanced at the house. "I assume he's inside?"

"Yep. Took off the minute I put the car in Park, maybe a second before."

"Was it that bad?"

"No. He did okay. Today was just about fun. We went four-wheeling. I even saw him enjoying it once or twice when he thought I wasn't looking."

"At least something went as planned. Are we still doing your training with Margo tonight?"

"I think we should postpone."

"What? Why?"

Behr motioned to where Nico and his daughter had just driven away. "Because the few minutes I overheard of that were emotionally exhausting. Ellery, hear me out. You can move Margo over to him. It would only make sense. He's ready for a dog, and I'm—"

Ellery covered her ears in full-on toddler mode. "Can't hear you. Not listening. Not going to happen."

The corners of Behr's mouth inched up like a parent who was both exasperated and unwillingly entertained by their child.

Ellery removed her hands. "Margo isn't a fit for Nico. He needs a smaller dog because of the rules at his apartment complex. At least he did last time. Plus, Margo's been trained for your type of injury and needs." She steamrolled ahead before Behr could fight back but softened her delivery. "And I'm not ready to give up on you with her. You can do this, Behr."

"Okay." His palms lifted like he was raising a white flag. "You're the expert. But maybe we shouldn't continue *tonight*. Give yourself an evening to regroup." His kind caramel eyes disarmed her. "We could push off our sessions until next week, when you're not training a new class of veterans."

"I'm afraid if we do that you'll have too much time to overthink and disappear. Escape Mt. Vista with only the clothes on your back just to avoid me and the very hard thing I'm forcing you to do. Well, the hard thing your family started, and I've continued."

A smile spread across his face, gaining momentum like sparks igniting kindling. "I would never. I would never disappear to a beach that didn't allow dogs and bury my feet in the sand."

"And I would never show up to said beach with Margo in tow." Actually—Ellery *would* never. If this experiment with Behr and Margo didn't work, she would move on. She would accept that. But she wasn't at that point yet. They were just getting started. "I am going to regroup. I'm going to make dinner and decompress. And you're going to help me because it doesn't make any sense for you to head home and then back here in thirty minutes."

"I'm not adding to your stress level today, Ellery." The way he said her name—like he cared about her, like they were more than two strangers who'd met on Monday and then jumped into a strange week of highs and lows together— carried a level of intimacy and warmth Ellery hadn't expected. But then, they'd decided to be friends, right? Well, she could use a friend right now.

"You won't be. You can help cook. I need your assistance." She didn't. But she wanted the company. "So, let's make dinner and then we'll get to work." Ellery paused. "Unless... unless your significant other is expecting you." Why hadn't she thought to question that earlier? Maybe Behr had dinner plans with his girlfriend. Maybe she wasn't fond of him spending time at Ellery's, even though it was in the name of service dog training.

"Marina lives out of state. I don't have plans... and I can't believe I'm admitting that to you."

And Ellery couldn't believe how happy and relieved that made her. It was good his training with Margo wouldn't be disruptive of his relationship. And it would be nice to talk to another adult during dinner. All she got out of Fletcher was nonverbals or grunts along with the occasional complaint.

If Behr's attempt at refusing to stay for dinner had to do with any regrets he was harboring over his initial suggestion that they should jump straight from acquaintances to friendship, then he needed to bury those.

Because it was too late now.

Ellery had already latched on to the idea, and she knew to hold on when someone good came along.

So they *were* going to be friends, whether he liked it or not.

And friends? They ate dinner together.

Chapter Five

Behr considered Ellery's plan to surge forward with training tonight to be on par with jumping from a moving train, skydiving for the first time without a professional, or eating a half gallon of Rocky Road in one sitting.

Any option would level him, and he feared tonight was no different. And it wasn't because of Marina, like Ellery had hinted. He hadn't gone into any details with her on that subject, even though he imagined Ellery would understand—or at least pretend to understand—his commitment to Marina and the kids. His hang-up regarding sharing more with her was simply because Jake's memory and his family were too important to Behr. Yapping about them all the time would be like tossing around diamonds until they lost their value. Behr kept the Robinson crew and his relationship with them tucked close to his chest in an inside pocket that very few knew existed. He wasn't ready to dive into that part of his life, especially after a day like today.

Four-wheeling had been fun and exhausting. It had taken more out of Behr than he'd expected. His head was a five on the pain scale and quickly escalating, and his body felt jittery. Weak. Like he'd slammed too much caffeine and couldn't come down from the high… which felt like a low.

Yet another fun symptom.

"Can I grab a glass of water?"

"Of course." Ellery pointed to the cupboard, and Behr filled a glass and then popped medicine that would hopefully help.

"What's my job?"

The first thing Ellery had done when they'd walked into the house was corral Dash into the basement, though she'd assured Behr that Dash had as little interest in being near him as he did the dog.

Apparently, Dash was a recluse who was only now adjusting to Fletcher even though he'd been living with Ellery for almost two weeks.

It seemed Behr had found his spirit animal.

So many people liked to assure Behr that their dog was different. Kinder. Sweeter. Would never bite. That somehow their pet wouldn't detonate his stark and debilitating fear. It had always been distressing to assure them that his issues had nothing to do with their particular pet, and everything to do with the species in general.

He'd had people laugh. Act surprised. Feel sorry for him like he was missing out on the world's greatest gift. And while that may be true, it was incredibly refreshing to be with Ellery, who didn't question or doubt his physical reaction to dogs.

She hadn't even considered pushing him into interacting with Dash.

When she'd said he only had to get used to one dog—Margo—she'd meant it. He appreciated that about her.

"Would you rather chop veggies for the salad or set the table?" Ellery had toed off her colorful athletic shoes near the front door and now padded around her kitchen barefoot, wearing shorts and a pink sleeveless shirt that tied at her waist. Comfortable in her element.

"Table." Behr could mess up a salad. Dishes, hopefully not.

"Plates are there." She pointed next to the glasses cupboard. "Silverware in the drawer below. Any chance you want to eat out on the deck?"

"That's a yes for me." Ellery's deck was shaded

by trees and built off the living room at the back of the house, overlooking the training center. Behr moved to the cupboard. "So, what else happened in your day besides Nico making you cry?"

Ellery retrieved a cutting board from a drawer and then a mountain of various vegetables from the fridge. She dropped everything onto the countertop. "I didn't cry."

"Maybe I'm thinking of myself then, because when I walked in and caught the end of his story and that silent sob thing he was doing…" Behr whistled. "About did me in. I don't know how you deal with that kind of emotional trauma from so many veterans. Must be exhausting."

She rinsed celery in the sink. "Most of the time it doesn't hit all in one day. Training weeks are like full moons. I never know what's going to happen."

"Sounds like training weeks are—" he paused for effect "—exhausting."

Whack-whack-whack. The knife moved at supersonic speeds as she chopped celery. "I know exactly where you're going with this, and I'm sticking by my earlier sentiment that giving you time to overthink would be detrimental to all involved."

She might be right. But he was also right to

think that adding his training on to her schedule during a week like this was ridiculous.

"I don't do it all myself during training weeks. I always have a veteran come in and talk about their experience and work through some of the issues they had when they first took their dog home. And my mentor, Goodrich, usually trains for at least half a day. He's retired, but he lets me rope him back in since trainings are spread out months apart."

"That's good at least."

"I'm not going to deny that training weeks are tiring, but they're also worth it. Seeing Nico like that was upsetting, sure, but I have to remind myself that he's heartbroken because Herman *worked*. Herman changed his life."

The way she couldn't resist selling Helping Paws—which really consisted of her—pulled a smile out of him. "Yeah, yeah, kid. I hear you," he said, striding toward the sliding glass door with the place settings and the silverware.

"Not that I'm trying to convince you or anything," she called out just as he stepped outside.

The evening temperature was hovering at seventy, and birds were chirping and flying around the yard like they were playing tag. Behr deposited the plates and set the table, then returned inside.

"You'd never do that."

"Never." Ellery scooped sliced carrots, snap peas and celery and tossed them on top of the mixed greens already in the bowl. "Hope you don't mind a mixture of things in your salad. I like to get creative with them." She started peeling an avocado.

"I'll eat anything." Especially after some of the food he'd lived through while deployed. Anything was better than MREs. Behr paused next to Ellery in the kitchen. "What do you need me to do next?" Somehow, despite her long day, she smelled good. Fresh. Like something citrusy.

"Drinks would be good. I have water or milk."

"I'm good with water. You?"

"Same. I'll check with Fletcher in a sec about what he wants to drink."

Behr filled a new water glass for Ellery and topped his off.

She finished the salad and set it aside, then removed the inside of the Crock-Pot with hot pads. It was filled with some sort of chicken and sauce that smelled like garlic and home. Behr had tried to refuse dinner when they'd been down at the training center, but now that he'd inhaled the scent, there was no going back. She snagged a serving spoon and moved toward the deck while carrying the chicken.

He cradled the salad in the crook of his arm so that he could follow her with the glasses of water. But like a one-year-old, he stumbled over the rug in the living room, sending moisture splashing over the rims.

Ellery reappeared in time to catch his misstep.

"Don't tell me Margo could've helped me with that."

She grinned and mimed zipping her lips. Behr continued outside to drop off the items. By the time he returned, Ellery had already soaked up the spill.

"Sorry about that."

"No problem. I'll just grab Fletcher and then we'll eat." She pounded down the stairs with an ease that caused a bout of jealousy in Behr. The simple act of moving, of coordination, which he'd always taken for granted, was now at the top of his wish list. And it would likely never return to him fully.

The doctors had said he should be thankful to be alive. To not be in a comatose or vegetative state. Behr was. But he still allowed himself the occasional moment to mourn an activity that used to be elementary and now required concentration.

Ellery returned at a much slower pace. "Fletch

is going to eat later. Says he's not hungry." She scooted past him, escaped to the deck.

Behr followed and paused with his hands on the back of the chair opposite her as she took a seat. "It's because of me. Just let me go so you two can eat in peace." They were blurring the lines too much for the kid. Behr understood it. He'd been torn over staying for dinner because of those same concerns. And torn over staying for training because his current exhaustion level was at ground zero and sinking fast.

"Nope."

"You're like a toddler today with the ear coverings and the nopes."

"He'll be fine." Ellery placed a napkin across her lap. "I've tried placating him, and it doesn't work. At this point he's going to have to give a little."

She was probably right. Behr could see how hard she tried with Fletcher and how standing up to him in small ways like this could be a good thing. Ellery was showing Fletcher that he wasn't going to be able to throw a hissy fit and get his way.

Behr's sympathy went out to this woman who was attempting to be Storm and Captain Marvel and Black Widow combined. Dealing with a broken veteran earlier and another broken one across the table from her, plus running a charity, plus doing her best to love her spicy teenage nephew.

She was pretty amazing. If Behr weren't so focused on Marina and the kids, he could find himself switching directions. Find himself wondering how to support Ellery and all she had going on.

But I'm not the only one of us who's attached.

True. They both had plenty on their plates. So, while Behr could be friends with pretty, intriguing, big-hearted Ellery Watson, that was as far as things could go.

The goal today was to introduce Margo to Behr again, but this time in the same space, no crate. When Ellery had left Behr in the training room just now in order to leash up Margo, she'd felt the nerves pouring off him even though he'd buried any physical reaction.

She was torturing him. And yet, if this worked in the end, his quality of life would greatly improve.

She just had to keep focusing on that. Was this what parents felt like when they disciplined their kids? It was for his own good, but the front-row seat to Behr's suffering in order to achieve the end result was excruciating.

Ellery leashed Margo and walked into the training room with her.

Behr was sitting on the bench that lined the wall, raking his hands over his khaki pants from hip to knee on repeat. Since he'd come straight from work to drop off Fletcher, he wore an evergreen Step Up polo, khakis and laced boots. Ellery had always thought polos registered as functional and not the least bit attractive, but somehow Behr demolished that theory. He could look good in a torn T-shirt. Covered in mud. With an allergic reaction climbing his face. It could turn out to be problematic, that zip, that attraction that registered in her gut. But she wouldn't let it.

He massaged his closed eyelids and then ran his fingers through his wavy chestnut hair, making it stick up in a few places. Endearing. And tired. Definitely tired. He reminded Ellery of a kiddo ready for nap time.

"Hey." She softly warned him of their approach, not wanting to surprise him.

They'd have to keep things short tonight. Just a friendly introduction—hopefully with Behr and Margo managing a closer proximity than last time.

She took a seat a few feet down the bench from Behr, keeping Margo tucked against her far hip, her body a block between them.

"Sit."

Margo obeyed, eager to please. Ellery kept a

tight grip on the leash. The last thing she needed was Margo ecstatically bounding over to greet Behr, shoving him over the edge of panic.

A sheen of moisture lined his forehead.

"How are you doing? Okay?"

He inhaled shakily. "Yeah. It's so frustrating. Embarrassing, really. I wish I could turn this part of me off."

"I think it makes perfect sense. If any civilian had been through the scenarios you had, they'd have the same concerns and issues. You're not doing anything wrong, Behr."

"Feels like it. My heart's about to blow right out of my chest." His hand mimicked an explosion.

"I can crate her for a bit. Give you some time to calm down, and then we can try again."

"No." Behr's head shook resolutely. "What were you going to do next?"

"I thought if she chilled between us like she did the other night in the crate, it might be a good next step. I won't let her get close enough to sniff or touch you."

Behr rolled his neck from side to side like a boxer about to enter the ring. Only this battle was with his internal monsters.

"Do it."

He was obviously pushing himself past his comfort zone. Was that smart? Or would it backfire? *I should have found professional help for him. I have no idea what I'm doing.* Slow was the name of the game in Ellery's opinion. But if Behr didn't push a little, this could take months. Years.

"Margo." The dog's ears perked.

Ellery directed Margo, and she switched positions, lying down between Behr and Ellery. "Stay. Good girl." Ellery gave her a training treat and made sure she had the leash cinched so that if Margo got the idea to say hi to Behr, she'd be stopped short of reaching him.

Behr's back was made of steel and glued to the wall, his focus straight ahead. Wasn't there a Bible verse about not veering to the right or left? He had that down pat.

"If you have any intel about how today went with Fletcher, I'd love to hear it. If you feel comfortable talking about it in here. We would have ample warning if Fletcher were to appear for some reason."

Behr hadn't filled her in over dinner because he'd been concerned about Fletcher overhearing. He didn't want to destroy any chance for trust to develop between them in the future.

Smart. But Ellery was dying to know more… and hoping to distract Behr. She wasn't going to get any info from Fletcher, so Behr was her only opportunity.

"He didn't talk much, which isn't a surprise. Although I think that us focusing on doing something fun did shock him. While we were on the golf cart, I gave him a quick rundown about MENtor camp and what to expect. Explained some of the buildings and activities and rules. He was quiet, but I do think he listened. And the rest of the time we were on four-wheelers, so there wasn't a lot of deep conversation. He definitely has an adventurous side. And a cautious one, too, I was glad to see. He took a bit to get adjusted to the machine before checking out how fast it could go." Behr's mouth formed a short-lived half-moon. His shoulders were still squared off with the wall, and he still hadn't so much as glanced in Margo's direction. "Don't worry. We have them set with throttle control so they can't go too fast. After, I took him over to the stables to show him the horses. He met Raven, a high-school-age girl who works in the stables. Pretty sure he thought she was the best thing about Step Up."

"Fantastic." The last thing Fletcher needed to focus on was a crush. "How come Step Up has a cute girl working in the stables? Shouldn't they know teen boys have the attention span of a gnat?"

Behr laughed. "I still resemble that description. And yes, they do. Raven was only there because her family takes care of the horses. She usually works outside of the hours the boys are on site, but no one else was there today but us, so we surprised her. I told Fletcher she's off-limits."

"Which will only make him more interested."

"Maybe. Maybe not. I suggested to Fletcher that he steer clear of girls and dating during the two weeks he's doing the program, because one, he won't have any time for that, and two, we need all of his attention. He acknowledged that with a grunt."

Not a surprise. Sometimes Ellery considered texting Fletcher even when they were in the same room and she had a question because she was more likely to get an answer.

Margo shifted, causing the leash and collar to clink and Behr to jump in his seat.

Ellery winced. She'd take the blame for that, but Margo had barely moved. She couldn't expect the dog to be a statue.

"How would you feel about a walk outside?" She asked Behr. "It's a nice night, and my street is pretty quiet in the evenings. I'll keep Margo on my left and you stay on my right. At least that way we're doing something to distract you and occupy her."

"Nothing distracts me." Behr popped up from the bench, paused about five yards away and did an about-face. "Even with her lying there, I'm on high alert. My adrenaline is straight fire. I can't do this. It's too much. I just…can't."

He stalked out of the training room, leaving Margo and a stunned Ellery in his wake.

"Welp. *That* went well," Ellery snorted. Margo plunked her chin on Ellery's knee in solidarity and support.

"Thanks, Margo-girl. You're not doing anything wrong, you know. Just like Behr isn't. It's just…this is a tough one. Okay?"

Margo nestled closer, bringing comfort.

At least when Ellery failed at helping Behr adjust to his dog, she would always have the other veteran success stories. She should focus on those. But all she could see was Behr's hunched shoulders and his stark dejection.

That image would haunt her all night.

Chapter Six

Freshly showered and feeling a million times better than the night before, Behr downed a swig from the travel coffee mug riding shotgun in his Subaru Crosstrek.

His headache from last night had dissipated while he'd slept, and his system, which had been pushed to the max while four wheeling yesterday, had calmed. Reset.

Which left him with the memory of his hissy fit and exit from Ellery's last night.

Embarrassing. Awkward. Mortifying. All of the above.

The morning sun momentarily blinded him, and Behr donned his sunglasses for the rest of the short drive to Ellery's.

At her front door, he knocked quietly instead of using the doorbell so that he could avoid bugging Fletcher. And avoid explaining to the teen why he was here and how last evening's session had just…imploded.

On Monday, Fletcher would start MENtor camp with one hundred other boys. Behr imagined Fletcher's excitement levels over that were nonexistent. He understood it. Most teens wouldn't want to spend two weeks of their summer learning how to be a better man, but then, Fletcher's behavior had left everyone around him very little choice.

No one answered, so Behr knocked again. This time barking followed. Maybe Ellery was already around back, at the training center. He knew she had the last group training session today, which was why he'd driven over here on his way to work, wanting to get this out of the way, hoping not to interrupt her classes.

Fletcher opened the door, Dash joining him. Behr moved back involuntarily. Dash stayed put next to Fletcher, but that didn't quiet the rat-tat-tat resembling a machine gun coming from Behr's chest. Didn't help that Ellery's dog resembled a wolf with piercing blue eyes.

"She's around back." Fletcher's voice was raspy and full of teenage accusation, his nonverbals insinuating that Behr had woken him up. He was surprised Fletcher could recognize him through his shuttered lids and the hair that had to be stealing any remaining portion of his vision.

"Thanks." Behr looped around the house and down to the training center, navigating the inclined driveway at a snail's pace and once again wishing someone would have tucked balance into his Christmas stocking. He wasn't sure if bumping into Fletcher outside of Step Up would grow their relationship or deter it. But there really wasn't another option since Ellery was training him with Margo. Their worlds were going to intersect on more than one level.

Behr and Fletcher's individual battles both felt too big and too insurmountable to attack from the human level, so Behr was trusting that God would somehow quiet his stark fear of dogs and somehow reroute Fletcher's current wayward trajectory. And that whatever Behr's role was supposed to be in Fletcher and Ellery's lives outside of his position at Step Up, God would show him.

Behr stepped into the training room. No sign of Ellery. The ruckus coming from the kennel area left little doubt as to her whereabouts. He inhaled like he'd just surfaced from thirty feet under water, but his core still trembled.

He couldn't leave without talking to her. Even if it meant dealing with canines before he'd finished his morning coffee.

Behr knocked on the door that led to the kennels. No way he was walking in there without knowing if they were unleashed.

"Ellery. It's me." *It's me.* That statement held a high level of familiarity. How was it possible they'd only met a handful of days prior? Behr felt like he'd lived a thousand lives in the span of this week. He'd certainly experienced that much fear in that short amount of time.

Ellery peeked out. "Hey." She moved into the training room, shutting the door behind her. "What's going on?"

"I came to apologize for last night."

"No need for that."

"I disagree." An apology *was* needed, and it meant more in person. Ellery was going above and beyond for him. He was the one who'd botched it all up.

"Behr, everything that happened last night was my fault."

Not even remotely close to true. But her delivery eased his tension. "I mean, I didn't want to be the one to say it but…"

"I know!"

Humor surfaced. "I'm messing with ya, kid. Last night was nowhere near your fault." She was way too quick to blame herself for just about anything. "I should never have stayed. I was exhausted from four-wheeling, and I didn't want to admit it to you or myself. I don't like that my body isn't what it used to be." Behr's father had raised him to detest weakness. Behr appreciated all he'd learned from Dad's lessons about hard work and perseverance, but ever since his injury, weak was the only label that fit him.

"I'm the one who pushed you to stay. You said you were tired. You said we should delay the session. I was the one who didn't pay attention to the details."

"If I'd been more open with you, I have no doubt you would have. It's just…it's hard for me to admit I'm struggling sometimes." Or all the time. It was hard for him to dive to this level with Ellery, too. He didn't even disclose this stuff to his sisters or his buddies or Marina.

"I get it. You have to fight for things that previously came easily to you. Anyone would feel frustrated by that, Behr."

"So you're not afraid of me because I lost it last night?"

Ellery's laugh, which he'd first filed under four-point-five stars—would listen to again— was quickly morphing into one of Behr's favorite sounds. She was generous with it. She spread it around like confetti at a birthday party or cookies during the holidays.

"If that's your version of losing it, you're

going to have to put on more of a show. Does this mean…are you calling it quits with Margo? I wouldn't blame you if you did. Not after the terrible experiences you've had here."

Behr wouldn't label any of his experiences with Ellery as terrible. Just unexpected.

They were both hard on themselves. He didn't see how any of this was Ellery's fault. He was the one who couldn't bear the company of an animal who had the power to assist him.

Was he done? Or did he have another go in him? Last night his body had basically shut down when he'd gotten back to his place. He'd dropped into bed and then ended up sleeping with the light on all night because he hadn't had the strength or coordination to get up and turn it off.

So simple, and yet, impossible for him in that moment. He knew based on some of the additional videos that Ellery had asked him to watch that this would be a task Margo could have done with ease.

Yes, Behr could live without a service dog, but he was curious to know if he could figure out how to live *with* one. With Margo.

"If I quit now, you would be riddled with guilt since this was obviously all your fault."

"Obviously." Ellery's smile grew bright, entertained.

"So I guess we'll have to give it another try."

Her exhale was long and relieved. "Good. And I'll figure out how to make the next time go better."

"Don't put that kind of pressure on yourself. Neither of us know what we're doing. We're figuring it out as we go along, and that's okay. We don't have to be perfect at this. There's nothing wrong with trying and failing and then trying again." At least that was what he was attempting to believe about himself.

"Again with the counseling sesh."

"You owe me ninety dollars."

"That was only a two-minute session, so I'll count last night's dinner as payment."

"Deal."

And hopefully the deal he'd just made to continue training with Margo wouldn't backfire again like it had last night. Because Behr wasn't sure how much more of his own weakness he could handle.

"I think you should go purple."

Ellery was in the salon chair, her friend Brynn standing behind her. "Whatever you think. I trust you." She checked her phone for the hundredth time, waiting for a call or an email to materialize. Nothing. Usually she couldn't get her phone to stop chiming and beeping, but now that she was desperate for that? Nada.

"Hmm. How about neon pink then? Definitely neon pink."

Ellery placed her phone on the countertop and made eye contact with Brynn in the mirror. "Did you say neon pink?"

"Right after I said purple. I was trying to get your attention." Brynn raised a perfectly manicured eyebrow. With bronze skin, ethereal blue eyes and a spot of star-shaped vitiligo covering half her forehead, Brynn was strikingly beautiful. She used to cover the lack of pigment with makeup, but in recent years had stopped, having decided to rock her body exactly as God had made it.

Brynn began applying color to Ellery's hairline—the same auburn as before, thankfully—her hands quick, efficient. "You've been *gone* ever since you sat your booty in my chair. What in the world is on your mind? Is this about Fletcher disappearing the other night? I'm sure he was just blowing off steam. I doubt he'll make a habit of it." Brynn continued to work through sections of Ellery's hair. "Did he get into that camp thing you were talking about?" The salon was filled today since it was Saturday, but each chair was portioned off from the next, creating a slight barrier.

"He did, thanks to Behr. It's going to be so good for him. I hope. And Desiree is ecstatic about it." Ellery had been relieved about that. At least she wasn't the only one ready for some reinforcements when it came to Fletcher.

"Then *what* is going on? You were thinking about Hot Veteran, weren't you?" She pointed at Ellery's reflection. "I should have known. That should have been my first guess."

Ellery had been thinking about Behr, but not in *that* way. Ever since the Thursday evening fiasco, she'd been intent on figuring out better ways to help him adjust to Margo. She'd contacted Goodrich, her mentor who'd trained her on all things related to service dogs, and asked him for advice. Had he ever gone through anything similar? Did he have any suggestions?

Goodrich hadn't dealt with a case as severe as Behr's, but he'd given Ellery the contact info for a psychologist in Denver who worked specifically with cynophobia.

Ellery had left a voice mail for Dr. Kapp yesterday and followed up with an email. Overkill. But since she and Behr were attempting another training session this afternoon, she needed help. Wisdom. Advice. Anything.

Brynn began adding color to the back of Ellery's hair. "Did you kiss him? You did, didn't you? You kissed Hot Veteran."

Ellery groaned. After she'd filled Brynn in on her plans to train Behr, her friend had demanded photo evidence. Because of Brynn's persistence, Ellery had been forced to look him up on "The Google" as her dad called it. It certainly hadn't been her own curiosity that had led her to find the *Mt. Vista Post* article about Behr's numerous awards and medals. It was for Brynn's sake that Ellery had gone down a thirty-minute rabbit hole of all things Behr online. She'd even found an article outlining the attack that had injured him along with seven other soldiers and killed four.

Painful, painful stuff that had helped Ellery to understand the man better.

Once Brynn had seen Behr's picture, she'd dubbed him Hot Veteran. Obviously she had no plans to let that label go.

"Nope." Ellery infused steel into her answer, hoping to derail Brynn's interrogation. Quickly. "It's not like that. Not even close. He has a girlfriend. And even if he didn't, mixing business with pleasure wouldn't be smart. I have a charity to run. And quit calling him Hot Veteran. Please."

A woman with white hair popped around the partition. "Did someone say something about a hot veteran? I've been married to one of those for fifty years." Her eyes twinkled. "I couldn't help but overhear as I was walking by."

Ellery and Brynn's amused gazes collided in the mirror.

Good for her keeping the spark in her marriage, but did that mean they had to dish to her?

"Hot butter," Brynn filled in. "We were talking about seafood dipped in hot butter." She pointed to Ellery. "New recipe she's trying."

"Oh." The woman waved her hand. "Carry on then. Not nearly as interesting as the subject I thought I'd overheard." She continued walking with her stylist to the sink. "How strange. Usually my hearing is spot-on and I don't miss anything, even from across the room. I wonder if I need to get it checked."

Ellery grimaced, making Brynn quietly snicker. "Quit laughing!" she whispered. "Now she thinks she can't hear!"

"I'm sure she'll figure out her elephant hearing is just fine. We need to get some music going in here or something. It's almost like I can't have a heart-to-heart with my girlfriend anymore. The whole town wants to know what's up."

"Hair & Now is always slammed on Saturdays. But trust me when I say there is nothing to tell about Behr. Nothing to dish. Unless you want the details of how terribly our last training session went." Ellery's frown reflected back at her. "Not that I haven't obsessed about that enough. I actually called a psychologist Goodrich recommended who specializes in Behr's phobia, and I'm waiting for him to return my call. *That's* why I'm so distracted."

"I'm glad to hear you may have found some assistance with HV's training, but it's still a bummer he has a girlfriend."

HV. Only Brynn. "Actually, it's great for him to have support like that." And if Brynn met Behr, she wouldn't be surprised to find he had someone. Ellery certainly wasn't. The man was the equivalent of fancy-pants chocolate behind a fancy-pants display case. And that combination of stubble, those teasing butterscotch eyes, that strong frame…he didn't exactly turn her stomach green.

"Fine. Be supportive and sacrificing and all Ellery-like."

"It's what I do." It wasn't, but Brynn thought Ellery gave too much of herself, her time, her energy to Helping Paws. Or just to other people in general. Not a dialogue Ellery wanted to resurrect right now.

The conversation turned from Behr to other things—Brynn's work, both of their families, Fletcher, Helping Paws.

Brynn had just finished the color and added

a cap when Ellery's phone rang. She lunged for it. "It's the psychologist!" Excitement propelled her out of the chair.

"I guess we're done here," Brynn said dryly.

"I'm going to go outside to talk to him." Ellery swiped to answer as she made her way out the door. "Dr. Kapp, thank you so much for calling me back."

"Just Kapp, and I'm happy to. I've known Goodrich a long time. What can I do for you?"

Ellery had left bits and pieces on his voice mail and outlined more in the email, but she gave him the CliffsNotes version of Behr's story.

"I really want to help him, but our first couple sessions haven't been the greatest. Well, I guess the first wasn't too bad." At least when it came to the dog part. "But the last one was pretty tough."

Enough silence greeted Ellery from the other end of the line that she was afraid Kapp had hung up.

"I would suggest starting exactly how you are—baby steps. There are a few different immersion avenues you can try. I can send you some information. Normally I wouldn't do that without meeting him first, but it sounds like you have some time sensitivity in getting him set up so that his dog can help him. And like you're already on the right road."

The right road. That was encouraging!

"If it would help, I'm happy to offer him some assistance and meet with him. No charge."

"Really? That would be amazing."

"My father was a marine, and I'm always looking for ways to support our veterans."

Kapp was too good to be true. "Thank you so much. I'll talk to Behr and we'll get back to you if he's interested in that, which I hope he is." Professional support would be a godsend. "In the meantime, it's nice to know we weren't completely off base in how we were attempting this."

"Patience is going to be key. If traumatic events led to this, it will take trust and time to change that."

After thanking him profusely, she disconnected, and Ellery returned to Brynn's spot in the salon.

"Well?" Brynn peeled back Ellery's cap to check the color. "What did he say?"

"He said we're not as off-track as I felt. He's going to send me some information, and he also said he's happy to talk with Behr."

Ellery did a little dance in the chair, and the white-haired woman who'd stopped by earlier paused on her way toward the exit. "Hope you have a lovely dinner and your recipe turns out!"

"Thank you." Ellery waved. "Have a great night."

Brynn's shaking shoulders were a dead give-away of her rising amusement. Thankfully, the woman's vision wasn't as hawklike as her hearing.

Once she'd left the salon, Brynn laughed until tears pooled. "I don't know why I'm finding this so funny!"

"I'm craving seafood now."

"Ha!" Brynn calmed down after a few deep breaths and a couple swipes under her bottom lashes. "Sorry—got a little distracted there. That is really great news about the therapist. I'm glad to hear it."

"Me, too. It's a huge relief."

"Now let's get you rinsed. You're cooked, and you've got a Hot Veteran to meet for a training session."

Ellery rolled her eyes.

Brynn just laughed harder.

Chapter Seven

"I hate this." Behr refused his sister's unnecessary assistance and shuffled solo to the sofa.

"You're a grumbly Behr today." Alessandra grabbed a blanket and brought it over to him as he settled on the couch.

Behr set it aside. He wasn't ninety. He just couldn't seem to stop breaking himself.

"You'd be a grumbly bear, too, if the people you asked for help actually made things worse."

"Drama!" Alessandra waved a dismissive hand and moved into the kitchen. "I'm getting you a glass of water."

"Lots of ice, please."

Her head poked through the kitchen opening. "Don't you think I know that?"

Rap-rap-rap. Three quick knocks sounded on his door. "Now, who would that be? Girlfriend you haven't told me about?"

This day was getting worse by the second. "Nope. Marina lives out of state. You know that."

"Who isn't your girlfriend, but who you're attached to as if she were. Even though she's not."

He nodded, then regretted it. "Exactly."

"Don't say *exactly* when that makes absolutely no sense, Behr Delgado."

He wasn't going down the Marina road again with his sisters. That topic was closed, which he'd told them numerous times. As usual, they didn't listen.

"You don't have to get the door. Probably a salesperson."

Alessandra was already there, swinging it open.

"Hi, I'm Ellery Watson. I'm sorry to stop over like this—"

"Why?" Behr yelled from the sofa. "Not like you haven't done it before."

He heard Ellery's huff and enjoyed it far too much before realizing why she was here. He was supposed to be at her place right now, training with Margo.

He should have texted her when he'd faceplanted three hours ago, but he'd assumed the ER and stitches wouldn't take one thousand years like they had.

"I'm sorry that I was *worried* about you, Behr Delgado!" she piped back.

"Come in, little spitfire. Come in." Alessandra stepped back from the door to make space, motioning for Ellery to step inside. "Anyone who sasses Behr-Behr is an instant friend of mine."

Could Alessandra be any more embarrassing right now? Next time he needed help Behr would call an ambulance. And spend five years paying off the ride.

Alessandra shut the door behind Ellery. "I'm Alessandra. Behr's older sister."

"I'm the baby," Behr chimed in. "You're all my older sisters." He took every opportunity to remind each of them that he would always be younger and look younger, no matter how many potions and lotions they used.

"You got that baby part right." Alessandra shot him a look that said, *Sit up, talk nice, quit your sassing.* As the *oldest*, she was good at those looks. "I am my parents' crowning joy." Alessandra placed a hand against her chest as she spoke to Ellery. "Their firstborn. Smartest. Wisest. You get the picture."

Ellery's cheeks creased. "I absolutely get the picture."

"This is Ellery," Behr reintroduced her, and Alessandra clapped her hands together.

"The dog lady!"

"Her name is Ellery, not the dog lady." Behr didn't share with his sister that he'd referred to Ellery that way in his mind at first, too. She was on probation right now for what she'd put him through this afternoon.

"Ellery. Great name. Sorry. Didn't mean to call you the dog lady."

"I've been called worse." Ellery broadcasted no offense, but Behr kind of wished she would. Was it wrong that he'd enjoy witnessing Alessandra's penance?

"How serendipitous that you're here." Serendipitous? Alessandra was laying it on like buttercream frosting. "We're all dying to meet you. And we're so excited about Behr being matched with a service dog. Of course now you know he didn't want to be, but since when does anyone in our family listen to anyone else?"

"Preach." Behr tucked a pillow behind his back.

Alessandra ignored him and continued. "I was just grabbing Behr some water. I'll grab you a glass, too. Be back in a sec." She popped into the kitchen, leaving Ellery standing by the front door like she was stuck between the two spaces.

"You thought I was quitting on you without saying anything, didn't you?"

Her teeth pressed into her peach lip and then released. "No. Maybe. I don't know." With each admission, she stepped further into the room. "I thought maybe that last bit with Margo had pushed you more over the edge than you'd even realized."

"And I was late, and you were counting the seconds."

"Not seconds."

"Minutes."

"Maybe minutes."

"Wondering how I could be this much of a jerk…wondering why I hadn't said anything!" He did his Hulk impression again, which earned lilting lips and apple-red cheeks from Ellery.

"Rude!"

He laughed.

"What happened?" Ellery motioned to the bandage covering half his forehead and dropped to a seat on the coffee table, facing him.

He should embellish. Make the story better. "Alessandra whacked me with a baseball bat."

"I'm not saying you wouldn't deserve that," his sister called from the kitchen. "Because you might. But I most certainly did not." Behr's whole place could fit inside most people's living rooms, so of course she would hear everything they said.

"What actually happened?"

"Alligator."

Her eyes rolled. A Fletcher-ism she probably didn't even realize she shared with the teen.

"I tried to pick something up. Got off balance. Crashed into the door frame. Earned a few stitches. Not nearly as exciting as you might think."

He'd called Alessandra, hoping she would butterfly it or even stitch him up, being that she was a nurse. She'd refused and forced him to go to the ER. Her excuse? Something about her not being a practicing nurse in the last fifteen years. Hooey. She could have finagled something. Behr didn't need it to be pretty. Wouldn't be the first or last scar his body boasted.

"Sounds painful." Ellery leaned forward, her fingers tracing along the bandage.

She was incredibly close. In his space, but somehow not realizing it. Behr, on the other hand, was fully, *fully* aware.

"Is your head killing you?" She straightened as if her intrusion was normal. As if her running fingertips along his scalp was second nature.

"Not as much as my sister is."

"Pshaw." Alessandra poked her upper body out of the kitchen. See? Listening to every word. "I'm not in the mood for water. How about I make us some sweet tea, Ellery?"

"Sure, thanks. As long as it's not any trouble."

"No trouble at all."

"I'd take some water." His sister had obviously forgotten him in the excitement of meeting Ellery.

She shooed him like a fly. "Hang on, hang on." She disappeared back into the kitchen.

"You didn't have to stop by to check on me. You know there's this newfangled thing phones do now. They call *and* they text." Behr kept his volume low in an attempt to prevent his sister from catching every word. Not that there was anything to hide. But she would most definitely relay every bit of this encounter to his other three sisters and his mom.

"This coming from the man who showed up at my place yesterday morning." True. He had done that. Some things were better in person. "And speaking of, have you checked your phone lately, Behr-Behr?" Ellery eased close again, her voice teasing, her proximity distracting. "Because I both texted *and* called."

If he inched forward the slightest bit, he could silence those sassy lips with his. Not that he was going to dwell on that strange thought.

He dug in his shorts pockets and came up empty. "Less, have you seen my phone?"

She came barreling out of the kitchen with a tall glass of ice water for him, delivered it. "It may still be in my car. I'll check."

"I can—"

She popped out the front door before he could relay that he could look himself. He might have cracked the other side of his head open, but he could manage to walk out to the car.

He faced Ellery. "Sorry I didn't warn you in time that I had managed to come up with alternative plans for this afternoon."

Her smile was a match, igniting a flicker of heat in his gut. "Next time you're knee-deep in the ER, please remember to notify me immediately."

"Here we go." Alessandra came inside waving his phone.

"Well. Now that I know you're okay, I should go." Ellery started to stand.

"Oh no, you don't!" Alessandra held up a finger, sending Ellery back to her seat on the coffee table. "We're hanging out a minute. Stay." She entered the kitchen again, and Behr and Ellery's mouths curved in unison at the canine command.

"I'm starting to see what you were saying about your sisters being really, really great."

He snorted. "The best."

"Ellery, our mom and dad dropped off some sandwich fixings," Alessandra called from the kitchen. "It's too much for just us to eat, so you really should stay and have some with us."

Behr dug fingertips into his temples, and Ellery laughed again, that light, happy sprinkling of sugar she seemed to spread wherever she went.

"Thanks. I had lunch not that long ago, but I'll think about it."

Ellery's hair was styled differently. Softer or straighter or…something. "You changed your hair. I like it."

"I just got it colored today and my friend Brynn styled it. I never take the time to do it as well as she does." Behr didn't bother adding that it always looked good, even if that was the case. Because he wasn't going down that road with Ellery at all…and certainly not with Alessandra present. "You put another hole in your head and still notice hair. That is impressive, Delgado. Can't say I've ever met a guy like you."

He could say the same about a girl like her. If the first week he'd known Ellery Watson had been full of this many surprises, he could hardly imagine what the next few would hold.

Ellery had agreed to stay to eat half a sandwich with Behr and Alessandra, not because Alessandra had held her captive and refused to let her leave—though that wasn't the biggest stretch. She'd stayed because the more she knew about Behr, the better she could help him with training.

At least that was what she told herself.

And the idea that she wanted to be around his sister…the kind of family who showed up when you needed stitches. The kind who delivered food. The kind who bossed and scolded with so much love they'd jump through hoops to sign you up for a dog you didn't even want and couldn't stand to be around…that had nothing to do with it. Nothing at all.

Alessandra and Ellery were currently rinsing dishes and loading them in the dishwasher. They'd sent Behr off to the couch to rest, much to his annoyance. It was interesting to see him with his sister. He acted disgruntled, but in a teasing way. He obviously loved her very much. Loved his whole family very much.

Ellery dried her hands on the dish towel that hung next to the sink. "Thanks for letting me stay." *Or for practically forcing me to.* "It was great to get to know you."

Alessandra hugged her. "Of course! Same. Thank you so much for helping Behr like you are."

"I'm happy to." And she was. Ellery regretted that she and Behr had started his introduction to Margo during the stress of the past week. She should have waited until her group training was done like Behr had suggested. Because now that it had finished yesterday *and* she'd spoken to Kapp, she felt much more capable. More energized. This next week would be a fresh start. As long as Behr could handle training with his stitches. She imagined something like that wouldn't hold him back, though. Alessandra had told her over sandwiches that she'd practically had to rope and drag him to the ER. Behr had wanted to finagle a solution for the wound at home.

"Our whole family knows it's over and above. And it's our fault. I'm sorry we signed him up without his permission. We were oblivious as to how much work this would turn out to be. For you. For him."

"Then it's a good thing you didn't realize it, or Behr would never have been matched with Margo. I'm glad you broke the rules." Ellery checked her gut and found the assurance held true. Perhaps at the start she'd been frustrated by what had felt like a lack of respect. But now that she knew Behr and understood where his family was coming from, Ellery was thankful everything had happened the way it had so that Behr could get the help he needed. Hopefully. "Besides, I'm getting as much out of the bargain as Behr is. Did he tell you he got my nephew into his mentoring program?"

"He sure did not." Alessandra snagged a dish towel and dried a serving platter. Her nails were squared off and painted a bright, summer pink. "That's fantastic, Ellery. God bless that boy. He does have a brain."

"I can hear everything you're saying." Behr's dry retort came from the living room.

Ellery stepped out of the kitchen. Her cheeks were sore from laughing at Alessandra and Behr's antics. From enjoying the stories Alessandra had revealed about Behr, just like Ellery had hoped she would.

She'd found out he'd been the jokester of his platoon. Not a big surprise. And that he'd been a huge crybaby as a toddler. Behr had denied it, but Alessandra had shared enough stories to support her claim. It was wild to imagine Behr as the doted-on—and bossed-around—little brother of four older sisters when he was such a capable, strong adult who would never put up with that now. Or did he still? His sisters had signed him up for a dog he hadn't wanted. And he was going through with training of said dog.

It was also hard to imagine him not pitching a fit about the plays they'd made him participate in. Dressing him in various costumes. Directing him to sing or dance or relay lines.

Behr was in the chair, so Ellery sat on the couch. The same spot she'd occupied earlier this week. The first time she'd knocked on his door. Or knocked it down, as he liked to say.

"We weren't saying anything bad. I was just explaining how thankful I am for your help with Fletcher. Desiree is so excited about MENtor camp. She keeps texting me to say thank-you. I keep reminding her it was all you."

"She keeps messaging me, too. I really hope the program helps him."

"I think it will." Ellery had to believe it would. They all needed this win for Fletcher.

"We haven't finished discussing how you came over here today because you thought I'd quit on you and Margo without even so much as a text to let you know."

Ellery feigned innocence. "I would never think that." She'd definitely thought that. She'd also been a terrible friend to Brynn today at lunch. They'd scheduled her cut and color at the end of Brynn's shift so they could go out, catch up. But Ellery had spent the whole time jonesing to get home and read the information Kapp had sent. She'd been distracted and a no-good, very bad friend. Times ten.

Unsurprisingly, Brynn had accused her of thinking about Hot Veteran the whole time.

Untrue in the romantic sense. True in the Margo sense.

Ellery had already texted Brynn an apology

and received a sarcastic, funny GIF of forgiveness back.

The information from Kapp had been helpful and encouraging. She'd been so eager to incorporate his ideas into Behr's training and then so disappointed when Behr hadn't shown.

Five, ten, twenty minutes had gone by.

She'd gotten antsy. Then agitated. Then worried. Repeat. She'd texted him: Hey, did you forget about today? Thought we were meeting?

She'd waited a full five minutes after the text before calling him. No answer, of course. Now she understood why.

"*I* would never. If I'm done or out—if I can't hack it anymore—I'm not going to hide it from you. Not with all you're doing to help me out." He continued with an intensity that tenderized her heart. "I realize that I didn't show for training in the first place, but that was because I didn't know you then and I had no idea how to communicate with you about all of my dog issues."

"That makes sense."

"But I know you now. We're friends." Her lips bowed at the elementary definition of what they were quickly becoming. His followed suit. "That won't happen again. From now on, I'm an open book with you. If I'm tired, you'll be the first to know. If I need to delay a session,

I'll say it clearly. And if I get to the point that I can't do it anymore, I'll be honest with you about that. Deal?"

"Deal."

Since Ellery's family wasn't anything like Behr's, she'd forgotten what it was like to be on equal and supportive ground. To be noticed and seen and appreciated. Behr was a balm to her—to the distance between Ellery and her parents and the pressure to be a support system for Desiree and Fletcher.

Though it would be wise not to get too used to that feeling. Behr had his own support system. And while Ellery would be part of it for a short while, once they were done training, their alliance would most likely end. Even if their friendship was growing at warp speed.

Because Ellery doubted Marina would be cool with Behr continuing his relationship with the dog lady after they were done training.

If Ellery were in the other woman's shoes, she definitely wouldn't be.

"Ellery is really, really great, Behr." Alessandra dropped onto the sofa and deposited the fresh-from-the-dryer basket of towels and bedding near her feet. Despite his protests earlier, his sister had insisted—in front of Ellery, no less—that she was going to do a load of towels

and sheets so that he was "set for the week."
Behr had finally caved in order to stop having
the argument in front of one of the most capable
women he'd ever met.

He could change his sheets without toppling
over. Or at least he had before. Alessandra doing
his laundry, though she meant well, only served
to remind him of his weaknesses.

Especially after a day like today, when that
weakness had been so noticeable.

"You two seem like you could be a really
good match," Alessandra continued. "You balance each other out. Make each other laugh.
She's in tune with whatever you're thinking."

"You got all that from a couple hours, huh?"
He checked his phone. "You managed to go six
minutes after she left before bringing her up. I
had you pegged for two."

"I was giving you some space."

He released a short burst of laughter. Six minutes equaled space in his family, apparently.

"The two of you were in here leaning, whispering, talking like you've been together for
years. Of course I'm going to notice that."

Just like he'd known she would. "Actually, the
whispering was so that you couldn't overhear
every little thing we said. Because I assumed
you were trying to."

"Pshaw. I was not. Your place doesn't exactly lend itself to private conversations, you know."

Oh, he knew. He should have put the kibosh on Ellery staying to partake in the sandwich fixings Mom and Dad had dropped off. But how could he have done that? *Hey, Ellery, despite how much you've done for me, you can't stay because my sister will get ideas about us. And then she'll infect the rest of the women in my family with those same ideas.*

"Wait—did you already text Mom, Suzette, Jana, and Chantelle about this?"

"No." The answer was clipped. Defensive. Alessandra focused on straightening the edges of the towel she'd just finished folding.

"Which means yes." He couldn't believe her. And yet he wasn't surprised. "How do you even move that fast?"

"It was just a text. Nothing to it, really."

Nothing to it? She'd tossed a lit match into a dry, barren ditch. Behr wouldn't be surprised to find four texts on his phone asking for more details by morning.

"There is nothing going on between me and Ellery. She's helping me. I'm trying to help Fletcher. That's it. I need you to let it go and call off the horses you just let out of the gate. Please."

"I'm sorry!" Alessandra bustled over to his

linen closet and deposited a stack of sheets and towels. She'd already put his extra set on the bed earlier. "I was just excited at the prospect of you finding someone so wonderful. I can't help it if you two are like potato chips and onion dip."

Behr snorted. "I take it I'm the chips in that analogy." Ellery would be the allure, the extra, the reason for someone to take a chip in the first place.

Alessandra didn't disagree.

"I understand why you'd jump to conclusions." Behr would give his sister that. "I do get along well with Ellery." And he found a huge amount of satisfaction in teasing her…in seeing that flash of confusion cross her face as she dissected whether he was joking or not. In waiting for that light to dawn, that head to shake, those lips to give into a curve. How could he not?

"That's all I'm saying."

Not *all.* "I know you guys mean well, but the whole infatuation with who I'm dating or not dating has to stop. I also know you don't understand my relationship with Marina." *No matter how many times I've explained it to you.* "Jake was my closest friend. Being attracted to his wife is just weird, first of all, and second, neither of us harbor those feelings for each other. She needs someone to listen to her, to support her, to encourage her. And that's my job right now. Not to date. Not to get married. Not to focus on myself. Concentrating on Marina and the kids gives me some peace. Really the only peace I can find in the situation." Behr snagged his phone from the coffee table. "This is what it's about. Right here." He pressed Play on an old voice mail, and Marina's sobs filled the room.

"It's been a tough day, and I just needed to vent to someone so that I don't take out my grief on the kids. They watched so many movies today! I'm a terrible mom." More crying followed and then a few indistinguishable words.

"I saved that not to torture myself, though it can work for that, too, but to remind me to pray for them. To support them however I can." The message had been from four months ago. It dawned on Behr that he hadn't gotten one like that from Marina in a long time. She must be healing some, then. Thank God for that.

Alessandra wiped moisture from under her lashes. "Okay, Behr-Behr. You win. No more talk about your love life. Or lack thereof. I hope you know we don't mean it in a vicious way. We just want you to have someone to support you and vice versa."

"I know. And I have lots of love and support. It doesn't have to be romantic."

She gave a slow nod, her smile blooming.

"That's true. All right. No more bugging you about women."

Behr didn't believe her in the least, but at least she was trying.

Chapter Eight

The first three days of MENtor camp, Fletcher had held on to his angry, bitter persona with a tight grip.

But day four—today—Behr could see a small light at the end of an exceedingly long and dark tunnel. Something had shifted. Changes were taking root.

Fletcher was currently talking—actually engaged in the conversation—with a group of boys. All shapes, sizes, colors. It was a huge coup to see him bonding, to see the young men starting to trust the process, their mentors, counselors, speakers, each other.

Because it made sense routing wise, Behr had gotten into the habit of dropping Fletcher off on his way home from work. He'd gone in search of the teen and now stood back twenty feet, not wanting to interrupt.

He could wait.

The campers had done it all over the last few days—community service, fishing on the stocked Step Up pond, zip-lining, baseball, basketball. Fletcher had listened to funny, gifted speakers covering subjects like work and integrity and future planning. Today he'd even sat through one of the smaller breakout sessions that Behr had led about the army.

Fletcher's conversation with the other boys ended on a big burst of laughter and then they all split off.

Behr caught his attention. "You ready to go?" He was careful not to sound rushed. No reason to derail any progress Fletcher had been making.

"Yep." Fletcher slung his backpack over his right shoulder, and the two of them took off.

The first few rides home, Behr had made the mistake of questioning Fletcher: *give me the good, the bad and the I-could-live-without.*

It was a question his dad had asked over the dinner table growing up.

Behr had naively thought Fletcher would participate. But he'd only answered the bad and could-live-without parts, by default, because all he'd done for the first three days of the week was complain.

"What's up with the community service?

You're just like Ellery, making me work. That speaker today was boring. I can't believe I'm in class in the summer. It's worse than summer school."

Behr had stayed quiet, letting him vent, certain someday he'd understand why they had the boys serve as one of the first things they did at MENtor camp. Like he'd thought when Fletcher had complained about helping Ellery with the dogs, it was always good to do something for someone else. It took the focus off yourself.

On today's drive, Behr was tempted to ask Fletcher if MENtor camp was worse than juvie. Ellery had called last night to say that three of Fletcher's so-called friends from his neighborhood had been arrested and would likely end up in juvie since it wasn't their first offense. Desiree had considered it a huge answer to prayer that Fletcher was in Mt. Vista with Ellery and at MENtor camp with Behr instead of off getting into trouble. Ellery had told Fletcher about what had happened to his friends, and even though she'd reported to Behr that he'd only listened and grunted in response, she'd hoped that he would finally see he was at a crossroads. Hoped that the boys' situation would get through to him, spark change in him.

And maybe it had. He'd certainly seemed different today.

But then, Behr could be reading the situation completely wrong.

"Been in the car a full five minutes and no complaints yet." Behr glanced at the once sullen teen whose face had begun lightening. Was that because of MENtor camp or because he'd begun styling his hair so that it didn't completely block his vision? Tough call. "You feeling all right?"

Fletcher snorted. His grin was fleeting, but Behr caught it.

"Did something…did something *good* actually happen today?"

Silence reigned.

Ah. So maybe Behr had been overly hopeful about his progress.

"One of my sessions today was with a pilot. Captain Crew." Fletcher said the man's name in a manner that Behr knew all the boys used because that was how Captain Crew introduced himself. Like *hooyah*, only insert *Captain Crew* because his background was navy.

The fact that Fletcher was participating even in that small way was a really good sign.

"He's a funny guy, huh?"

"I guess."

Behr tamped down on any humor attempting to rise up. Of course Fletcher couldn't give too much.

"He said he always knew he wanted to fly.

Did you always know you wanted to be in the army?" An honest-to-goodness question? Behr steeled his face to hide any enthusiasm. "I mean," Fletcher continued, "before the army jacked you up."

"Before the enemy jacked me up. Yeah. I always knew. My dad was in the army until he reached retirement. I was definitely the kid who played with those little green army figures and mapped out battle plans."

"Those are *old*-school."

"Well, I'm old, so that's fitting." And with the way his body functioned now, Behr's age could be multiplied like dog years. Ironic. "What about you? Have you always wanted to be or do something?"

"Nope." A splash of anger or something close to it dotted Fletcher's reply. "Kind of hard to do that when I don't have a dad to show me anything."

Mine clearance would be less dangerous than navigating this conversation. "No doubt about it, that stinks." Behr waited a beat, the hum of the tires filling the space between them. "You're allowed to have your own dreams, Fletcher. If your dad were here, I imagine he wouldn't care if you went into the army, built houses or taught kindergarten. I'm sure he'd just want you to find something that interested you. That you could work hard at and succeed."

Fletcher looked out his window. "Okay."

"You know, you could ask your aunt about your dad."

"My mom tells me about him all the time."

"I'm just saying. She knew a different side of him."

"Yeah." Fletcher shifted his body to look out the window even more. Like he was cutting Behr off, just like he had during their first encounter in the training room.

Behr should probably count the conversation as over, but he couldn't resist imparting a little more encouragement. Even if Fletcher pretended not to listen, hopefully some of it would sink in.

"It's also okay not to know what you want to do yet. You're only fifteen. You have plenty of time. Part of the reason Step Up has so many guest speakers from different careers is to show you boys what all is out there. Things you may not have considered before. Just enjoy the process and don't stress too much about not having a plan yet, okay?"

Behr could feel Fletcher's scrutiny switch to him, but he kept his attention on the yellow line. Would the kid explode? Tell Behr to back off?

"Okay." Fletcher's answer was missing its

usual hints of sullenness and irritation. Behr resisted raising a victory fist in the air since that would *definitely* not be well received.

"What the—why is my mom's car here?" Fletcher jerked forward in his seat as they pulled into Ellery's driveway.

"She probably missed you and wanted to see you."

There was no listening this time. Fletcher was out the door in a millisecond, leaving Behr undecided behind the wheel. He was supposed to train with Ellery and Margo tonight, but if Desiree was here, maybe that changed things.

If they were having a family issue, he should just go. Stay out of it. But if he did that without talking to Ellery first…well, he knew what would happen then.

"Mom, what are you doing here?" Fletcher had barreled in the front door and was now standing in the middle of the living room, his stance wide, his flecked-with-fear coffee eyes jutting between Ellery and Desiree.

"No *hello, Mom*?" Desiree stood. Opened her arms. "No hug?"

Fletcher stood still as a statue. "What's going on?"

"I miss you. I came to see you since you are my *son* and all."

Ouch. Ellery was only an aunt, but when Fletcher copped an attitude with her, it still smarted and stung.

Desiree, somehow, stayed calm. Years of practice, maybe.

Since she'd come straight from work, Desiree was dressed in wide-leg slacks and a coral shirt that complemented her espresso hair. Ellery had always been jealous of her complexion because no matter how much moisturizer she bathed her face in, she could never mimic Desiree's dewy golden glow.

Fletcher moved to hug her but stayed silent. He was obviously still questioning why she'd shown up out of the blue.

When Desiree had texted Ellery this morning to let her know she wanted to drive down and visit—that she had something to talk to Fletcher about—Ellery's nerves had inflamed so much she'd had to pop ibuprofen halfway through the day. How could she blame Fletcher for having that same instinct and fighting that same unease? And he was right, too. Desiree did have something more than seeing him on her mind.

"I'm going to let the two of you talk," Ellery excused herself. Behr had planned to stay for training after work, but there was no sign of him. Had he left after realizing Desiree was here?

"Come sit by me, honey. Tell me what's new."

Desiree directed Fletcher over to the couch as Ellery exited the front door.

Behr was in his car, staring at the house as if determining whether he should be here or not. *I feel you on that. Me, too.*

Ellery walked to the passenger side of Behr's vehicle. She opened the door and slid inside.

"Hey." The car smelled like Behr—clean and crisp and attractive. Soap, deodorant or just Behr? He didn't seem the type to don cologne.

"Hey." His brows tugged together, communicating his concern. "Everything okay?"

"I'm not sure."

"Why do I get the feeling that whatever is happening in there is negating the good day we just had?"

"Because that's a legitimate apprehension. Desiree came down to talk to Fletcher because she's been offered a job in Florida. She thinks it might be a good chance for them to start over, for Fletcher to run with a better crowd. She said she's been looking for a while, but nothing has been a fit yet. It's not like they would be moving right away, but she wanted to talk to Fletcher about it because she has to give the place her answer within the next week."

"That's pretty big stuff."

"Yep. I'm worried about how he's going to react." Ellery warily studied the house, half expecting Fletcher to come flying out the door any second and stalk off. "I wish this hadn't come up until after MENtor camp was finished. I think the boys' arrest spooked her." Ellery massaged fingertips across her forehead as Fletcher's balloon filled with a big puff of helium. "I'm not sure a move is the best idea. I get starting over, new friends and all that, but at least in Colorado I'm close and can help out. And Mom and Dad aren't too far in Montana. Florida just feels like the other side of the world, even though of course I know it's not. And yet…it's nothing I have any say over. I'm definitely not planning to give my two cents, even if Desiree asks for it. She has to follow her instinct. And I've learned my lesson the hard way on inserting my opinion when it's not my life."

"Huh. Really." Behr's dry, teasing tone drew an unexpected laugh out of her.

"What? Your situation isn't the same."

His quiet chuckle filled the car.

"It wasn't like I chimed in about you moving or changing jobs or something."

"Nope. Just forcing me to work with a dog I'm petrified of."

"Used to be petrified of." They'd made some progress earlier this week thanks to Kapp's advice. "And I only gave you a little shove." Though she'd been leaning toward meddling, intrusion and all the rest she'd just claimed she didn't do.

The skin kissing Behr's butterscotch eyes crinkled with amusement.

"You were just…you were trying to mess with me again, weren't you? So annoying how you do that." And yet her stress level had decreased. "If they do end up moving, then I'll trust God that it's the right plan for them. Desiree would obviously have prayed plenty over this, and now that I know about it, I can do the same. I guess the idea of visiting a warm climate in the middle of winter wouldn't be terrible."

"Attagirl."

Ellery had been fully focused on herself and her family's issues since Behr had arrived. Now she studied him.

"How was your day?"

"Good day for me." Yet weariness weighted his answer. "And I'd say a good day for Fletcher."

"I want to hear about Fletcher. I always do. But right now, I'm asking about you." She poked him in the chest, her finger running into a brick wall. *Hello.*

"We had an issue with the website today. It crashed right when registrants were signing up for one of our fall retreats. Since it's usually on a first-come-first-served basis—"

"Except for Fletcher."

He grinned. Raised those sturdy shoulders in a flash of what-can-I-say. "Except for Fletcher. Everyone was frantic and worried they were going to miss snagging a spot. I spent most of the day on the phone convincing parents that we would get things smoothed out and assuring them there would be enough room for everyone."

"Will there be?"

"By the grace of God, hopefully yes. Jasper mentioned adding another weekend to our fall schedule if needed, so that should help, at least."

"Wow. Sounds stressful. I thought you said it was a good day?"

"I mean, compared to gunfire and sleeping on the ground next to enemy territory, it wasn't bad."

"When you put it that way…" How could Ellery complain about anything ever? "So, what happened with Fletch? Something good?"

"He talked about his dad a little on the way home."

"He did? I've tried bringing up Ace a couple times with him, but he never shows any interest. I finally decided it wasn't worth it and gave up."

"I'd say it's worth it. He's probably listening even when he's pretending not to be. He's frustrated not to have his dad around to give him advice. I think he was feeling a little alone or lost when it came to dreaming about a future or a career. I tried to encourage him to take his time. I'm sure your brother would have known what to say, how to help him."

"Ace was a great father for the short time he got to be one. He would have been all-hands-on-deck if given the opportunity. T-ball, soccer, whatever the sport or activity or school project, Ace would have rocked it." A smile sprouted as she imagined her brother interacting with teenage Fletcher. Would he have gotten frustrated with his kid? Certainly. But he would have fought to love him well even when he was prickly.

"Fletcher's still holding himself in check, and I doubt that will fully go away anytime soon, but I think we're peeling back some layers with him. The fact that he talked to me on the ride home was encouraging. And today he was hanging out with a group of boys. I'm sure it's good for him to see other kids who are dealing with the same stuff as him, growing up without a father. Some of our speakers have that same testimony, and they've done great things. Hopefully all of that will hit home with him."

"From your mouth to God's ears." Ellery had

been praying constantly while Fletcher was at MENtor camp. That God would get through to him. That he'd begin to change. It was encouraging to hear that might be happening. All thanks to Behr. And God. And Step Up.

"Since you had a stressful day, do you want to postpone training?" She wasn't going to make the same mistake she had last week. Especially not after Behr's stitches on Saturday. No doubt he was still experiencing residual effects from that.

"I'm tired but not demolished. I can handle another short session like we've been doing." One of Kapp's suggestions was to keep the sessions thirty minutes or less. That way Behr didn't get so overwhelmed. He could use all of his energy and focus to adjust to Margo during that time frame because he knew the training had a clear-cut ending.

It had been working.

"You promised to be honest with me."

"I am." Behr's mouth arched to support his assurance, and Ellery imagined, just for one teeny-tiny second, what it would be like if he were hers. What it would be like to kiss him in greeting at the end of the workday. To make dinner and decompress together. To have a person to discuss all the things with. To pray with. The image was ever-so-tempting but way out of bounds. Behr had been up-front with her about who held the lock and key to his heart.

The least she could do was respect that.

Chapter Nine

I can do this with God's help. I'm not alone in this battle.

The mantra that Kapp had assisted Behr in crafting replayed again and again as he waited for Ellery and Margo to appear.

Behr had done a session over Zoom with Kapp during his lunch hour on Monday, and it had been extremely helpful. He and Kapp had developed the mantra as a way for Behr to focus on something positive instead of the negative thoughts that usually brought him to his knees and played like a cable movie on repeat. Kapp was a Christian, too, so they'd incorporated faith into it. A reminder of how God was looking out for Behr. How Behr was, not for one millisecond, alone in this battle.

Ellery entered the room with Margo on a

leash. The dog's tongue lolled to one side, her open mouth and visible teeth mugging for him.

Better to think that than to remember those same teeth could be used to inflict damage.

Whenever Margo entered a room with him, Behr experienced highs and lows like he was rafting snowmelt. He feared that each attempt to muster the strength to fight his phobia would be the last. That each attempt would earn him the stamp of failure.

And yet, here he was again. He'd failed last week, hadn't he? He'd stalked out of this training room so fast his shoes had probably left a trail of smoke behind.

But because of Ellery and Kapp and God, he'd come back this week. Things had improved. Still were improving.

Wearing shorts, flip-flops and a simple white V-neck T-shirt, Ellery was the picture of summer and beach and sunshine. Her cherry hair shone along with her eyes. She was so excited he was doing better. The thought of disappointing her cut Behr like a combat knife.

She approached and held out the leash for him.

This effort is worth it. That was another thing he and Kapp had discussed. He wanted Behr to focus on the value Margo would bring instead of the fear. The good instead of the bad.

Margo stood by Ellery's side, her chocolate face toggling back and forth between them, questioning what she was supposed to do next. Waiting for his lead.

Behr reached out and took the leash. If Ellery noticed his shaking hand, she didn't say anything.

"I want to teach her to stand by your left side. That's it. She's just going to be there. We're going to take it slow." Ellery moved to Behr's left, leaving enough room for Margo to stand between them.

A tremble echoed through him, and Behr tensed his muscles in an effort to curb it.

Margo, on the other hand, would be the first image if someone searched the internet for the definition of calm.

During their training session on Monday evening this week, they'd moved at a snail's pace— first letting Margo sniff Behr, then having him pet her. She'd sat next to him while he'd held one trembling hand to her soft fur.

Eventually Margo had chilled so much she'd sprawled next to his feet. Seeing her relax had helped Behr the most. The fact that Margo was confident in her own right and didn't need him to instill that in her was a huge help. She was the first dog he was able to just be present with since his tours.

Ellery had definitely been right that Margo was his match. He couldn't imagine handling a needy dog. He was the needy one!

They'd also done a short session on Tuesday after work, during which Ellery had shown Behr various Margo commands by demonstrating them herself. Not as good as him doing it, but it had allowed him to watch, listen, learn.

"Heel." When he gave Margo the command and she obeyed, taking that spot, Behr's heart just about ricocheted out of his chest. *This effort is worth it.* Was it, though? He could get through life off-kilter, running into things, tripping, leaving items on the floor when they fell, willing his poor coordination to work instead of using Margo to create balance for him or grasp or retrieve things for him, couldn't he?

How's that working for you? You currently have twelve stitches in your noggin.

"Doing okay?"

"Yep." Except he'd just jumped off the positive bridge into the cold river of panic. *I can't do this. Why did I think I could do this?*

Time to swim back to shore. Kapp had also coached Behr to take deep breaths on repeat. At least three every time he was struggling. Which meant he wouldn't be doing anything but breathing for the next thirty minutes.

Ellery didn't say anything about his audible

inhales or exhales, but she had to know what he was up to. The weakness that plagued Behr rose up to ridicule him. It was hard to reveal this side of himself to Ellery, not that she hadn't seen it already. Hard to know that he couldn't just snap his fingers and make his body right again. Hard to remember that he *needed* this dog and that was why his mom and sisters had signed him up for one.

"You're doing great." Ellery's focus was on Behr, but Margo's tail wagged as if the compliment had been directed to her.

They both laughed, and the tension dissipated like a deployment care package.

"You, too, girl." Ellery offered Margo a treat. "Do you want me to put the balance harness on her so you can feel what it's like?" she asked Behr.

He gave one determined nod.

Ellery strode over to the storage cabinets that lined the back wall. She returned with the harness and knelt, sliding it on Margo, adjusting it. Behr should probably be watching how to do the same, but right now he was concentrating on standing next to Margo and not having his knees liquefy.

Ellery stood. "See what you think."

Behr gripped the handle, his knuckles turning white. The handle was the right height, and it did make him feel sturdy. Supported.

Like the woman beaming at him from the other side of the dog.

Just when he thought Ellery was going to ask him to walk with Margo—and he was considering it—the timer on her phone went off.

"Time's up!" She shut off the alarm. "You did so good, Margo-girl." Her teasing gaze met his. "You too, Behr-Behr."

"Alessandra is in so much trouble." Behr tentatively placed his hand on Margo's back. She held still, like she was holding her breath. Both the women in the room probably were.

He gave her a quick rub along her spine and then moved away.

Ellery brought Margo back to the kennel and Behr copped a seat on the bench that lined the training room wall, his pulse shifting from revving to idling.

When she returned, Ellery joined him on the bench. "You're making so much progress, Behr. Well done."

"I'm not sure moving at turtle speeds is called progress."

"When Fletcher changes at turtle speeds we consider it a win."

She had him there. "Maybe we should have kept going, then."

"Kapp told us to keep things consistently short in the beginning so you can put all of your energy into it and trust it won't go too long. It's working, so I don't want to mess with it."

"True."

His phone dinged, and Behr checked it. Marina. She'd sent pics of the kids at Jakey's birthday party. Him blowing out the candles. Some of Adira running around with the boys who'd attended.

"Is that—" Ellery glanced away. "Sorry. Didn't mean to pry."

"Here." Behr handed her the phone. "That's Jakey and Adira. Marina and Jake's kids."

"They're adorable. Where do they live?"

"Louisiana."

"You must miss them a ton."

"I do. I'm going to visit them in a couple weeks for a long weekend."

"That's great." She returned the phone to him.

"There's nothing romantic going on between Marina and me." Behr dropped the bomb without forethought. He felt weird not sharing more with Ellery after all they'd gone through together and all she'd done to acclimate him to Margo. "I know I implied she's my significant other, and she is, in a way. But she's also not."

"Okay." Ellery's eyes were inquisitive and yet

not abrasive, her head tilted in a way that said she was listening.

"Jake was…he was my Ace." He wasn't sure how else to describe it and was confident Ellery would understand that analogy. "We weren't *like* brothers. We literally became brothers. The kids are my godchildren. I love Marina as a close friend—as Jake's wife. Still. I can't think of her in any other way, and we've never had anything romantic between us. But when we lost Jake, I committed to her and the kids. To caring for them and supporting them. And I didn't feel like I could concentrate on anything dating-wise in my own world when hers and Jake's had been torn apart like that. Especially along with learning how to adapt to my new physical limitations. I just started letting people assume that Marina and I were together-together. Because it was easier than trying to explain our relationship or my commitment to her and the kids. My sisters don't even understand it. They've been bugging me about her, thinking it's more than I'm letting on. But it's not."

"Wow." Ellery sat back against the wall.

"Think that's weird?"

"Nope. I completely understand where you're coming from."

"You do?" He shouldn't be so surprised by

her response, but it was definitely the first of its kind.

"Of course. I mean, look at me. Look at this place." She motioned to the training center. "I bought this house not because I liked the layout, but because I could envision Helping Paws here. I saw the additional garage and knew I could make it work. I wouldn't be doing any of this if it weren't for Ace. I had to figure out a way to honor him. A way to channel the grief and the anger and the sadness into something good. That's exactly what you're doing with Marina and the kids, and I'm sure they need it. I have no doubt that your support and commitment mean the world to them. I can't imagine Marina's loneliness after losing her husband, her partner. Filling that void for her and the kids... I get it."

It was Behr's turn to collapse against the wall. "I'm not sure I've ever been more understood." He'd definitely never met anyone who got him quite like Ellery did...even when it came to understanding his commitment to another woman.

"Glad I could accommodate, kid." Ellery borrowed the Behr-ism, meaning what she'd said—she did understand Behr's reasoning, and she respected his decision to be there for Marina and the kids. But that only left her in more of a pickle because recently her attraction to Behr had been growing like weeds during a rainy month of May—despite her attempts to squash them with Round Up. Even if Marina wasn't his other half in a romantic sense, that didn't change the rules of the game.

Behr was still off-limits. She was still deeply entrenched with Helping Paws.

"The 'kid' thing doesn't work as well coming from you to me."

"Why not? I'm a year older than you."

Behr's face registered surprise. "Are you?"

"I don't even want to hear how old you thought I was."

His hands rose in defense. "Younger than me, for sure."

"Uh-huh. Right."

"I just explained the whole Marina situation to you, which I rarely if ever do with anyone. Why wouldn't I tell you the truth?"

Ellery *was* flattered that Behr had been so open with her. He obviously trusted her like she did him.

At least he hadn't been thinking she was in her forties versus her thirties. Ellery had sprouted a batch of wrinkles lately that were giving her age away and then some. One in particular was quite pronounced, like a wide church aisle through the middle of her forehead.

A stress stretch mark, she thought each night as she lathered on decadent skin cream and woke to find it exactly the same size if not sassier and more pronounced. And the soft skin under her eyes was as un-perky as a teen about to enter summer school. But overall, she took care of herself. She tried, not because it mattered what anyone else thought of her, but because it made her feel good.

"So, when's my next torture—I mean train-ing—session?"

"Tomorrow is good with me. The sessions are so short that I'm pretty open."

He winced. "Sorry. Can't. Family thing. My parents are grilling and having the kids and grandkids over."

"Oh, that's great." Ellery experienced a bout of jealousy and the strangest desire to join the Delgado clan. How weird was that? Perhaps it was just because it had been a long time since she'd seen her parents. They hadn't visited since last summer. And when she'd tried to pin them down for a date this summer, they'd been eva-sive. No matter how many times Ellery told her-self that their lack of interest in visiting wasn't due to any lack of love for her, she had a hard time believing it.

While Behr seemed to be surrounded by the

kind of family that wouldn't leave him alone, she wasn't surrounded by any at all.

Enough feeling sorry for herself! She had Brynn. And Desiree. And Fletcher. Though those last two needed more support than they could give.

Like she'd told Behr earlier, Ellery occasionally let herself daydream about how different things would have been for all of them if Ace had lived. Sometimes the reflections made her smile. Other times they ended in tears. But one thing was always the same—she wasn't as alone in a world where Ace existed.

"How about Saturday, then?" she offered. "That will give you a down day in between."

"Are you sure you want to work on the weekend again? I feel like that's asking a lot of you. It's okay if you have plans."

The reminder that they'd also scheduled a session last Saturday—before his injury had interrupted—and she'd not had anything social on her calendar outside of a haircut and lunch with Brynn, plus her usual catch-up work, chafed like that cute, cropped pair of jeans in her closet that refused to fit even when she dropped weight.

Ellery's whole world revolved around Helping Paws and now Fletcher while he was in town. Often, her weekdays and weekends blended together, and she was left wondering why most offices were closed when she was working.

Except for Sunday. She was religious about going to church and getting herself centered for the week. And she did her best to rest on Sundays or do something that filled her self-care bucket like a hike with Dash. Oh, what a wild and adventurous life she lived.

"Saturday is fine. No problem at all." Ellery didn't add that she looked forward to her training sessions with Behr or that they were highlights in her week. Just like she wouldn't be admitting to anyone that Behr not being in a romantic relationship had made her heart do obnoxious jumping jacks and vie for her attention.

Don't go there, heart. Behr and I are friends and that's all we are. Don't mess it up by starting a crush now.

Or by admitting she'd been harboring one all along.

Chapter Ten

"I have a strange request." It was Friday, and Behr was driving Fletcher home after a full week of MENtor camp.

The teen had to be exhausted from the busy days and the conversation with his mom last night. When Behr had left Ellery's yesterday evening, Fletcher and Desiree had been sitting on the deck, their body language shouting that their conversation was heated and tense. Behr had gotten out of there quickly after his training session, and he hadn't heard from Ellery since, so he didn't know what had been decided about Desiree's job offer. And asking Fletcher was off limits in Behr's opinion. He was giving the kid the space he would want if their roles were reversed. All of that to say, Behr should really wait to ask Fletcher this on another occasion. But Behr's family was already getting together tonight, so asking was worth a shot. Even if he expected to hear a resounding *no* from Fletcher.

"What is it?" Fletcher's attention was a rare commodity, and it was directly on Behr at the moment.

"My parents…" Behr gripped the steering wheel tighter. "I've told them a little about you and Ellery. They've taken an interest in you, and…they'd like to meet you. I'm having dinner there tonight."

Fletcher had been fidgeting with the hem of his athletic shorts, but his movements stilled.

"I'm not asking you to stay for dinner." Behr rushed to explain. "I just wondered if you'd be willing to stop by their house on the way home and meet them. I'm sorry. I know it's asking a lot. They're just very persistent." *Persistent* sounded better than *pushy*, but both descriptions fit. Though Behr knew his family's intrusion came from a good place. Once they'd heard about Ellery's nephew, his family had instantly begun praying for the teen. Even his sisters who didn't live in town were involved in the teen's story and rooting for him.

In the interest of full disclosure and due to the fact that Fletcher hadn't refused yet, Behr continued. "It will be my parents and my sister plus her four kids. My brother-in-law is out of town for work." His family had asked him to invite Ellery, too, but Behr wasn't sure their worlds needed to collide on every level. Dropping by with Fletcher felt fine. But wrangling Ellery into this meet and greet seemed like his family was attempting to shove them from the friend zone into the something-more zone. Behr imagined his mom and sisters were fond of that second option and would settle for the first after a chunk of time. Much like he'd had to convince them Marina wasn't his soul mate.

Fletcher still hadn't responded. Not a huge surprise. "Don't feel like you have to. It's okay to say—"

"Sure. I'll go." The boy's tone was smooth. No irritation. No upset.

"Really?" Behr clamped his tongue between his teeth. If Fletcher had agreed, why question it?

"Yeah." Fletcher didn't exactly sound ecstatic about the scenario, but Behr appreciated when people took his answer at face value, so he would do the same.

"All right. Thanks." Behr's parents had moved a few years ago from Colorado Springs to a wooded area in Mt. Vista. From the back deck of their log cabin house, they had a view of the small but pretty Mt. Vista Lake. It was one of Behr's favorite places, and he'd spent plenty of his recovery time there.

They drove the rest of the way in silence—probably a relief for both of them after the long week.

Fletcher peered out the windshield as Behr pulled into his parents' wide driveway with the three-car garage and an additional shed to the right. A basketball hoop was perched between the spaces along the asphalt, and the kids must have been outside playing already, because numerous bikes and other games were in a heap outside the shed.

They didn't make it two steps from the car before the front door opened and Mom popped outside.

"You must be Fletcher!" She approached him with open arms, her short, coffee curls bobbing, leaving Fletcher no choice but to engage in the embrace or block and duck. Behr swallowed a groan. Did his family have no boundaries at all?

After the quick hug, Mom stepped back and studied Fletcher like he was a famous painting or a prized possession. "I'm Lucia, but the grands call me Lita and you're welcome to use either one. It's so great to meet you. We've heard so much about you." Or at least as much as they'd finagled out of Behr. Fantastic. Hopefully, Fletcher wouldn't read too much into that and assume Behr had been spilling dirt about him when he'd been very careful not to do that.

"Come in, come in." Mom ushered Fletcher toward the front door. "Are you both staying for dinner?"

"No. Fletcher just stopped by to meet you guys and then I'm dropping him home." Behr had roped the poor kid into this visit. He wasn't going to break his trust by having him stay when he'd told him he wouldn't do that.

Mom's smile faltered, and her eyes took on that glint she'd passed down to his sisters. A we'll-see-about-that look. Which quickly morphed back into a bright, welcoming flash of white teeth.

"Either way, it's great to have you here, Fletcher." She opened the front door and motioned for him to step inside. "Let me introduce you."

Inside the house, Alessandra's teen boys occupied the stools that butted up to the kitchen island, and the two younger ones—ten-year-old twin girls—abandoned the game of Twister they were playing in the living room and ran to greet Behr.

"Uncle Behr-Behr!"

Alessandra could be blamed for starting the nickname when Behr was a toddler and continuing its use into adulthood. And now passing it on to the next generation.

Just as they were about to crash into him

and—Behr unfortunately assumed—topple him over, a shrill whistle sounded.

The girls screeched to a stop.

"Remember Uncle Behr needs us not to be bulldozers!" Alessandra called out.

The girls' faces drooped.

"Get over here. You're fine." At Behr's permission, they finished their approach and hugged him gently on each side, like he was a porcelain cup that might break under too much pressure. Behr appreciated Alessandra stopping them from running him down, but he wasn't quite so delicate.

"This is my friend Fletcher." Behr nodded toward the teen, and the girls gave small waves. "How was your day?" he asked them.

"So good! We spent it at Lita and Lito's, and we ate ice cream for lunch!" Selah filled him in while Nadine elbowed her in the side and shot her a what-are-you-thinking-revealing-that stare. Apparently the ability to communicate by animated expression spanned all three generations.

"Mom, seriously?" Alessandra joined them, hands landing on her hips.

The girls skipped back into the living room, either oblivious to the war they'd started or hoping to avoid it.

"We ate vegetables, too, honey," Mom chimed in. "They just forgot to tell you about that part."

Fletcher stood near Behr, looking completely lost. *This was a bad choice. What was I thinking? I should get him out of here.*

"It's great to meet you, Fletcher." Alessandra did her impression of Mom's "Welcome!" smile. "I met your aunt the other day, and she spoke so highly of you."

"Nice to meet you, too, ma'am."

Look at Fletcher bringing out the big guns with the *ma'am*. Acting all respectful when Behr had expected him to grunt and nod and escape as soon as possible.

"Teenagers!" Alessandra called out. "Humans are interacting! Join us!"

Case and Rome dropped their phones onto the island in unison. They knew better than to disregard their very enthusiastic mama.

"This is Fletcher." Alessandra introduced her boys after they approached. Case was older at sixteen and Rome was fourteen. Rome was built like a linebacker, and Case was lean and long like a beanpole.

Case made eye contact with Fletcher and nodded in greeting, having recently grown out of the awkward middle school years. Rome, still firmly entrenched in them, only managed a mumble, his focus sliding no higher than Fletcher's Vans high-tops.

"Why don't you three boys head outside and see if Lito needs any help with the grill," Alessandra suggested. "And if not, then find something to occupy yourselves that does not involve a screen. Climb a tree. Basketball. Skateboards. Bocce ball. That beanbag game."

"Less, we're not staying. I just told Fletcher that we'd stop by and meet—"

"It's okay. I don't mind."

Behr's mouth borrowed one of those *O*'s that Ellery was so fond of. Fletcher didn't mind? Was he feeling okay? What was going on?

"Come on, Fletcher." Case strode to the front door. "It's best if we just give in."

"It's so annoying when they banish us from the house." Rome followed his brother. "Why don't the girls ever get sent outside?"

Fletcher trailed in their wake. "Do they do this a lot?"

"You wouldn't believe how much." Case's reply traveled back to them as the front door swung shut.

The girls were enthralled in their game in the living room—one not involving screens and likely the reason they were allowed to keep playing—so Behr took the opportunity to confront his very pushy sister and mom.

"You wouldn't believe how often my family says one thing and then does something completely opposite." Behr's voice had a growl-ish timbre to it that he had no plans to tone down. "I told you guys that Fletcher wasn't staying. I just stopped by to introduce him to you." He held up his phone—it was open to the text he'd sent at a stoplight on the way, after Fletcher had agreed to this torture. "I have it in writing. And you, Less, responded to it."

"I think I smell something burning." His sister took off for the kitchen like she was the fire chief and the safety of Mt. Vista depended on her.

Behr followed, as did his mom. He copped a seat on one of the stools lining the island that the boys had just deserted and waited for Alessandra to explain. Or make excuses.

Shockingly, the kitchen was *not* on fire.

"That was a thumbs-up text. That's like saying I read this, not like signing a contract. And I didn't force him to stay. He agreed to hang out for a minute with the kids. And once they're done, it will be time for dinner. When he smells the meat on the grill he won't be able to resist. Hunger is a teenage boy's number one emotion."

That part was true. "I can't keep him for dinner, Less. I don't even know what he and Ellery have going on tonight." She'd offered to train

Behr with Margo this evening, but that didn't mean her whole night was free. Their sessions were short.

Alessandra grabbed a carrot from the veggie tray and popped it into her mouth, then took her time chewing. If she snagged another one, Behr was going to knock it out of her hand.

She swallowed. "I actually already called her and convinced her to join us. She'll be here around six."

"You invited Ellery for dinner. Without asking me."

"Uncle Behr, come play Twister with us," the twins called from the living room.

"In a minute," he called back. Though Twister probably wasn't his best option—he'd likely end up going face-first into a sharp object. "I can't believe you invited Ellery over and are going to wrangle Fletcher into staying when I told him we were just stopping by. You're making me look bad."

"If he wants to go home, Case will drive him. No big deal."

"You have an answer for everything, don't you?"

"I do."

"Mom? Are you involved in this, too?"

"No one is involved in anything, honey." Mom had begun mixing a pitcher of lemonade.

"We just wanted to meet Ellery and Fletcher. And thank her for all she's doing for you. That's not a crime." She stirred the mixture quickly. "We're not meddling. We're just welcoming Fletcher and Ellery into our home. There's a difference."

Nope. Behr really didn't think there was.

Despite Lucia and Alessandra's warm welcome and consistent attention during dinner with the Delgado clan, Ellery knew something was off. Like neon yellow partnered with a soft, delicate pink, the kaleidoscope of colors didn't mesh. Behr wasn't comfortable with her being here, and she never should have come.

If not for his family being the most welcoming on planet earth, Ellery would have left fifteen minutes after she'd walked in the door.

Fletcher, on the other hand, was faring like he'd known Case and Rome since they'd all been in diapers together. They'd disappeared downstairs after dinner to play a video game that Ellery didn't have. She didn't have a gaming system at all. That had been one of the things that had delighted Desiree about Fletcher visiting her. Now that he'd found this haven of good food and good people plus video games, Fletcher was never going to be home. He might as well move into the Delgados' basement instead of hers.

"What a gorgeous night." The rocking chair next to Ellery that Alessandra occupied on the huge wraparound front porch creaked quietly with each push. "The boys should be outside. I think I'm done with the gaming." She glanced Ellery's way. "Do you have a preference?"

"Nope. You're in charge. And I doubt Fletcher's mom would ever argue in favor of a screen." Ellery sipped from her lemonade glass and returned it to the small metal side table, then resumed rocking. Everything the Delgado family chose for furnishings seemed to focus on comfort. Simplicity. Ellery wouldn't be surprised to find out the rocking chairs she, Alessandra and Lucia currently occupied had been made by hand. By a family friend of the Delgados. Who'd gifted the set of chairs to them out of pure adoration.

After dinner, Ellery had thought she and Fletcher should leave, but with the promise of dessert on the horizon and Lucia and Alessandra dictating her schedule, she'd been ushered onto the porch. And once she'd taken a seat, had never wanted to leave the oasis that was the Delgado compound. Mature, gorgeous trees filled their lot, their summer greenery fluttering in a faint breeze. They'd decided to sit along the front of the house since it was currently shaded, versus the back porch, now sheathed in the hot, setting sun.

"Then I shall rouse the troops." Alessandra's perfect white teeth flashed. It was almost as if she relished ripping the boys from their favorite pastime. She stood. "Do you two need anything? Mom?"

"It's time for dessert, don't you think?" Lucia pushed up from her chair. "Dad will want a little coffee to go with the cookies." Mr. Delgado— Sal—was quieter than Ellery had expected. While Behr was constantly teasing, joking, his dad was more serious. But over dinner, he'd been very kind and interested in Ellery's work. His features were so similar to Behr's. Even their builds were identical. Ellery had felt like she was looking thirty years into Behr's future.

"I'll help." Ellery wasn't just going to sit here and be served.

"No, no, no." Lucia waved both hands. "You sit! Enjoy the view! It's only palmeritas. Nothing to it. I just didn't put them out earlier so the kids wouldn't devour them."

Lucia and Alessandra bustled into the house before Ellery could protest more.

"I should follow them." Ellery pressed the toes of her leather flip-flops into the deck and sent the chair rocking. "But they'll just shoo me out of the kitchen." Ellery could get used to this view, this company. Being at the Delgado household felt like being on vacation or being waited on at a bed-and-breakfast.

When Alessandra had called to invite her, Ellery had caved easily at her insistence because she'd wanted to experience Behr's family. And they'd been every bit as wonderful as she'd expected they would be. She'd let herself be convinced by Alessandra even though her instinct had said that if Behr had wanted her here, he would have said something yesterday.

Ellery was certain she'd inched too far into Behr's world. It didn't matter that his family had been the ones to rope her into coming. It mattered that Behr hadn't and she'd come anyway. And now things just felt awkward between them. They'd barely spoken to each other so far tonight. Either she was overreacting and reading into that, or she'd crossed an invisible line that she now couldn't find in order to backtrack over and return to normalcy.

Her overanalyzing was interrupted by three grumbling teenage boys. They poured down the front steps of the house and over to the shed, not even noticing that she was sitting on the porch. They were too distracted by the injustice of having to turn off their video game. And yet... Fletcher was smiling.

They retrieved skateboards from the shed—what activity didn't this household have?—and began working on tricks. Or whatever the moves were called. Ellery knew Fletcher had an interest in the sport because he'd brought his skateboard to her house, but he hadn't used it yet. It stayed on the floor in his room like a prop.

None of the boys were going to get a sponsorship anytime soon, but they were having fun.

Fletcher made a botched attempt at a trick, gave a yelp and landed on the driveway. He writhed on the ground, holding his ankle. Ellery sat forward in her chair. Should she go to him or not? Would that be embarrassing?

"Mom!" Rome yelled. "Mom, come here!"

Alessandra jogged out the front door and over to the boys. Ellery followed her at a distance, praying Fletcher was okay.

"Did you twist it?" Alessandra knelt by him.

Fletcher gave one nod, his jaw tight with tension. Likely intent on not appearing weak with Case and Rome.

Much better that a nurse check him out versus his aunt. Ellery didn't want to baby him too much, but of course she was worried. It was never a good thing to break someone else's child. She backed up to give them space and bumped into Behr. Instinctually she reached out to steady him.

"It's going to take more than you to knock me down, kid." His mouth eased into that teasing grin of his, his eyes crinkled, and suddenly her world righted.

"I could put some shoulder into it next time." Behr had some inches on her in the height department, but their difference wasn't so much that it would say…take effort to kiss him. He was right there. Within reach.

And yet so out of reach.

"What happened?" He nodded toward Fletcher, who was still being triaged by Alessandra.

"I'm not even sure. They were doing something on the skateboards, and he just went down. Ankle, it sounds like."

Behr winced. "Whenever I turn an ankle, it makes me nauseous."

"I think we need to ice it and you'll be right as rain in a day or two," Alessandra announced. "Just a little sprain. Boys, help him inside and we'll ice it and have dessert at the same time."

Case and Rome supported Fletcher on each side, and he hopped into the house, leaving Behr and Ellery staring after them.

"It really is helpful that your sister is a nurse. I wouldn't know what to do in this situation, and she just handles it."

"Except when she refuses to stitch someone up and makes them go to the ER."

"You're a little bitter about that, aren't you Behr-Behr?"

"I really am."

"After watching Alessandra handle that, I'm feeling the need to add someone with a medical background to my circle."

Behr laughed. "Is that how you choose your friends? Based on their professions and skill sets? Do you accept applications or just add to your people on a situational basis?"

"Situational basis."

"Then how did I make it in? What do I bring to the circle?"

"Hmm." She pretended to think, though the answers came quickly. *Consistency. Kindness. Friendship. You care about me. Notice me.* Perhaps that was why when she'd arrived tonight and he'd been aloof—at least in her mind—it had smarted like baby smooth skin against pavement.

"If I'm ever in need of avoiding a sniper attack, or—" she lifted a finger "—the knowledge of how to survive in the wild for days or weeks on end, I feel like you'd be my go-to."

"So I'm your wilderness survival guide?"

"That sounds about right. I'll get you some business cards and a name plaque."

Ellery tucked the flash of amusement she earned from Behr into her stash of favorite things.

He nodded toward the porch. "Let's sit and let Alessandra handle him. She's a pro with stuff like this." He paused. "As long as you're okay with that?"

"I'm great with it. I'm sure Fletcher would prefer her clucking over mine." They moved to the rocking chairs, which Ellery couldn't resist sending into motion. Lucia had been outside at some point, it seemed, because a small plate of cookies was perched on the table between the chairs.

Ellery took one and so did Behr. They were the perfect blend of flaky and crunchy and melt-in-your-mouth.

"It's gorgeous here." The lot that housed the log cabin home was private. Quiet. A sanctuary, really. It reminded Ellery of her favorite over-look in the hills surrounding Mt. Vista Lake. Which should really be classified as a pond, but in Colorado, any water was a commodity.

"This porch is one of my favorite places. I lived here for a bit with Mom and Dad after my injury, during recovery, and the porch—front or back—was my grounding spot. I would do my devotions out here or just listen to music. My parents were amazing and helpful after my injury, but I was so ready to move out. We were all ready for me to move out. Living with your parents as an adult is not easy. On either side of that equation."

"I get the impression that you moving out after your injury would be harder on your mom than your dad. Am I way off?"

"She was worried about me. It's what moms do. Although, she works hard on letting us go. She isn't a guilt tripper. She always says she raised us to fly, so clipping our wings doesn't make sense."

Two squirrels chased each other through the branches of an aspen. "I like that. If I ever have kids, I'm adopting that model." Kids. Ellery hadn't entertained that idea in a long while because she'd known she would need a partner to make that happen, and the partner hadn't materialized. So she'd just…stopped considering the option.

Years ago, she used to get asked out. But her work had become so important to her that the phone calls or texts or interest from the male species had stopped. It was likely they saw the closed sign on her forehead. The way she had poured herself into Helping Paws and only focused on it was probably a deterrent. But Ellery couldn't help it. Even now, she wanted it to succeed so badly. She wanted to help more and more veterans. More Aces and Jakes who did get to come home. What were their lives worth back in the States if they couldn't acclimate to them? Couldn't really *live*?

"Have you ever been in a serious relationship?" Behr's question surprised her, but then, why should it? She'd practically tossed the subject out there like a whiffle ball pitch over home plate.

Ellery hadn't talked about her relationship with Trent in years, but she knew she could trust Behr with it.

The question was whether she wanted to or not.

Chapter Eleven

"Yes. Right when I was starting Helping Paws." It was amazing how Ellery's voice held steady even though she was shoveling to unearth something she'd prefer remain buried. And yet, Behr had let her into his secrets, the nooks and crannies of his injury and trauma. How could she not be honest with him in return?

She continued. "We talked about getting married, but then things shifted. Trent became disgruntled with how much time I was devoting to Helping Paws. It was all consuming back then. I was new to everything, and everything took a ton of time and effort. I assumed that he would come alongside me with the charity. Support me. Support it. That he would understand how much it meant to me because I was honoring Ace."

She'd thought that he would grasp that Helping Paws was way beyond a charity or a career or even a mission. It was her actual beating, bleeding heart. But he definitely hadn't seen it the way she did.

"He grew more and more irritated by my lack of attention—that's what he labeled my drive and determination to get Helping Paws up and running—and eventually ended up giving me an ultimatum." It was why Ellery was so careful now to tell people up-front that she was in a relationship with Helping Paws. Because the crash and burn of that union had wounded her at levels she didn't even admit in her most introspective moments. She'd moved on by pouring even more of her energy into her work. At this point, she wasn't even sure how to extract herself or regain a level of normalcy. That was why she understood Behr's commitment to Marina and the kids so well. They were basically doing the same thing in a different way. They were loving the ones they'd lost, in the best way they knew how.

"Wow. He made a terrible decision, and yet I'm glad you didn't end up with him." Behr had stopped rocking and was tenderly watching her. "He didn't deserve you." Ellery's heart bobbed into her throat like a flotation device careening to the surface, making it hard to swallow. Trent had never looked at her anywhere close to that way. No one had.

"What about you?" Suddenly she wanted the attention off herself. And quickly.

"Nothing big to tell, really. Have I dated? Sure. During the short stints that I was stateside. Did I ever think any of those brief relationships had a future? No. Women don't love the idea of a guy who isn't home ninety percent of the time. Turns out they like their partner to be someone who's around and not deployed. At least in the scenarios I encountered."

"Weirdos."

Behr grinned. Nodded. "Exactly. I think most of the soldiers who were married in my platoon married young. Or they knew their spouse before enlisting. So maybe it's more of a joint decision in those cases. I'm not sure, but none of my relationships ever panned out."

She shouldn't be so relieved, so happy to be reminded that Behr was *technically* single. Just like she shouldn't be harboring a growing crush on the man. Especially when she'd just reminded herself of exactly why *she* was single.

"So…" She borrowed one of the calming breaths she'd noticed Behr doing during training. "I have a question."

"All right. Shoot."

"Was tonight uncomfortable for you because I

was here? I'm sorry about crashing your family dinner. I could have said no when Alessandra called." Though it would have been as tricky as resurrecting one of her deceased houseplants. Canines Ellery understood. Green things that grew out of dirt—or were supposed to grow— not so much. "Actually, I tried to say no, but Alessandra is *very* convincing." Ellery *had* tried to say no. At first. But she'd given in far too quickly because of her aforementioned desire to be part of the Delgado family. To be part of something that was rare in her world.

Behr set his chair in motion. "I wasn't—I'm not uncomfortable because you're here. I'm always glad to have you around." Well. That was nice. "If I seemed off, it's because I don't like when my family is so pushy. I assumed Alessandra had basically forced you into this, and I didn't want you feeling that pressure. You're allowed to have a life outside of Helping Paws and training me with Margo."

Ellery's relief was swift. It wasn't about her. It was about his family. "But here's the thing… I don't have a life outside of Helping Paws. And I'm okay with that at the moment. It's just where I'm at right now." *It's where I've been for years.* Ellery fought a wince. She'd chosen this—or at least it had chosen her. She didn't want to change any of that, did she? "Your family might seem pushy to you, but to me they're just inclusive and welcoming. I like it. I like being around them." *And you.*

Ellery wasn't sure why her family couldn't or didn't function like Behr's. Had Ace been their glue and they'd fallen to pieces without him? Maybe. Probably.

"If you like this crew, then you should come when everyone is here. Between my other sisters, I have another four nieces and five nephews. When we all get together, it's a madhouse."

What would it be like to join one of those gatherings, to be part of the Delgado clan? Yes, they stuck their noses in each other's business, but they also cared deeply for each other. It was visible in their interactions—in their pushiness, as Behr liked to label it.

Ellery loved her little family. She just wished they were more involved in each other's lives… and that Ace was still here. Always, she wished for Ace.

"Desiree asked me to apologize to you for last night. She said she naively thought that the idea of moving might be a relief to Fletcher. That he might welcome a fresh start. She hadn't realized that having a discussion about the option would backfire so completely."

Behr snagged another cookie. "She doesn't

need to apologize. She didn't do anything wrong. Talking to Fletcher makes sense. How could she know how he'd react? One day he might be excited, the next upset."

"Exactly. I relayed all of that to her. I just hope she listens and accepts it. She's doing her best for Fletcher. She always has. She was just worried that she derailed Fletcher's progress at MENtor camp."

A loud burst of laughter came from the house, then some rambunctious voices. Ellery recognized Fletcher's participation and a puff of helium leaked out of his balloon, easing the pressure inside her. They were getting somewhere with him, like Behr had said.

Slow was the name of the game with Margo training *and* her nephew, it seemed.

Behr angled his ear toward the house, the corners of his mouth lifting. "Sounds to me like he's doing all right. I had the same thought at first last night, but then I realized one conversation shouldn't mess up everything he's learned. If anything, what Fletcher's being taught at MENtor camp should help him deal with unexpected stresses like that. It's part of the program to learn how to roll when things don't go as you anticipate."

"Desiree told Fletcher that she would refuse

the job offer in Florida. And while he was still slightly sullen this morning, he did thank me for buying the cereal he likes for breakfast. Earlier in the week, he was so disgruntled over having to wake up early during summer break that he barely spoke to me in the mornings. So maybe he is using his new tools and handling things better than he would have in the past."

"Attaboy. I'm glad they figured things out. Is Desiree okay refusing the offer?"

"She is. It was never about her and always about a fresh start for Fletch. They talked about the need for him to find different, better influence friends in Denver since they're planning to stay, and he seemed to understand that."

"That's great progress. Sounds like the upsetting conversation for him actually led to something good."

Very true.

"By the way, did Fletcher ask you about camping next weekend?"

Camping? "No, he didn't. Why, what's going on?"

"The boys who don't get to stay overnight at the ranch for MENtor camp are doing a one-night camping trip next Friday. It's kind of a celebration-graduation thing, and I'm one of the chaperones. Earlier today I tried to get a read on if Fletcher wants to go, but he didn't say much when I asked him. I thought maybe you could feel him out. See if you can tell."

"I'll do my best. Desiree and I had both hoped he'd open up more with me while he was here."

"He might not be an open book, but he wouldn't have let me swing by to introduce him to my family a week ago. And I definitely don't think he would have stayed for dinner or got along with the boys so quickly. He might be holding out with you, but he is changing. Hopefully with more time and more coaching, he'll let you in."

"You're right—even if it's not directly with me, any changes are good. Seeing him with Case and Rome tonight was a huge win. I got emotional twice watching them interact."

"You big softie."

Like he was one to talk.

Ellery had started the evening unsure of her place and ended next to the person who was quickly becoming her safe place. And his family was a soft spot to land, too. Ellery respected Behr's commitment to Marina and the kids so much, so she was just going to be thankful for his friendship…and not get greedy with his time or support. That way, if or when their new-found relationship dissolved at the end of training Margo and mentoring Fletcher, she'd still be able to float and survive on her own without the life raft Behr had quickly become to her.

Right?

Right.

In true Delgado fashion, Mom had roped everyone into playing charades after dessert. Most families would have let Fletcher escape to nurse his wounds. Behr's family did the opposite, holding the teen and Ellery captive even longer.

The game did seem to lighten Fletcher's mood. It looked like he'd all but forgotten about his ankle for most of the time, only wincing when he tried to stand to take his turn, then bowing out due to the injury.

Behr assumed he preferred it that way, and no one had pressed the teen. On that at least.

Ellery and Fletcher had just left, and Alessandra was loading up her car now.

She popped back into the house. "We're taking off." She hugged him, then stepped back. "I'm sorry for orchestrating. I didn't mean to. It just comes naturally to me."

"That was a terrible apology."

"Yes. But also, I was kind of right! I mean, how amazing was tonight? The boys got along great with Fletcher. I think they already made plans to hang out this weekend."

It was the worst when Alessandra was right. Did Behr actually have to admit her meddling had resulted in good?

Her smile bloomed like he'd spoken that out loud, but to her credit, she didn't hound him for the admission.

"I'll see you later. Call me if you crack your head open again." The front door closed after her. Behr's sigh filled the house. And to think, Ellery *wanted* a family like his.

Behr wandered onto the back porch in search of his parents and found Dad occupying one of the Adirondack chairs, a cup of decaf perched on the armrest. He was nothing if not predictable, but Behr wasn't naive to what a gift that was. His dad was a constant. Quiet? Sure. Strong? Absolutely. Easily rattled? Never. Always there for them no matter what? Without a doubt.

"Hey, Dad." Behr took the chair next to him. He'd been planning to leave, too, but time alone with his dad was a rare commodity.

"You have a nice friend there, Behr."

"Yep."

"She's doing good work for a lot of veterans. I respect that. A lot. I was just sitting out here thinking of friends who could have used a service dog over the years. So many lost. So many to suicide. It's hard to adjust after... Well, you know."

He did.

They sat in silence for a few minutes. Behr felt the peace of his family and the comfort of home tugging on his eyelids.

"She makes you happy."

His eyes popped open. "What?"

"Ellery. You laugh a lot when you're with her."

"We were playing charades, Dad."

"We did more than that. There's joking and there's joy. And you were in the second category tonight. I know my son." That sentiment both warmed Behr and dipped him in a freezer. Because if Dad could see into his mind, then he'd also unearth Behr's growing attraction and attachment to Ellery.

"It's not like that."

"I'm not saying it is. Yet."

Seriously? Had Mom and Alessandra put a bug in Dad's ear or something?

"No one put me up to this." Again, the man was reaching in and stealing his thoughts. "Your mother thinks I'm not listening half the time, but I am. I'm also seeking some space to form my own thoughts. And these are mine."

Huh. Who knew Dad could be so eloquent? Half the time he didn't speak. Or he didn't have the space to speak. Someone else in the family was always talking.

"All I'm saying is that you seem comfortable with her. Like she makes sense in your world, your sphere. That's it. Just…don't lose that. It's rare."

Mom stepped out onto the porch just then. "Hello, loves." She brushed a hand along Dad's arm as she passed to take the chair beyond the two of them, a quiet, simple gesture, and yet it gutted Behr. Had anyone ever been so tender with him outside of his family? Any women he'd dated in the past were a strong no. But Ellery was like that with him. So careful, so protective of him around Margo or even Dash. And yet she didn't let him wuss out without trying, either. Was Dad right? Did she bring joy to Behr's world?

Of course she did. But that didn't make them a match like Dad had implied. And yet…now his mind was spinning.

If Behr's mom or sisters had relayed what Dad just did, Behr would have disregarded it. Because they'd been butting in, inserting their opinion for years.

But Dad…he'd never expressed anything like that at all.

Chapter Twelve

It was the kind of summer evening that made Ellery fall even more in love with Colorado. The temperature was a perfect seventy-two, the sun reaching for the mountains but still lending heat, and the sky the kind of blue that should earn its own crayon color.

The Mt. Vista park she and Behr had agreed to meet at after work on Tuesday wasn't large, but it had a smooth pathway that curved around it. A perfect spot for Behr and Margo to attempt their first public outing.

In the two sessions since dinner at the Delgado house, Behr had advanced in his training and his trust of Margo. He'd even given Margo a quick rubdown after each session. It was always from the side, never face-to-face, but he would pet her back if she stayed still and didn't make any sudden moves.

Ellery could tell the action took huge effort on his part. He'd told her about the mantra he and Kapp had come up with, and the breathing exercises, which she'd witnessed him using.

For all the fear he had to tread through to make these sessions happen, he was a star pupil and incredibly determined. If Behr wasn't so strong, he would have given up long ago.

Ellery exited the vehicle and Margo stayed in the truck until Ellery gave the signal for her to follow. It was an important part of her job—waiting until her owner was ready for her.

Behr parked his Subaru and approached from the other side of the park as Ellery slipped the balancing harness onto Margo. He wore khaki shorts and a heather-green shirt that complemented his olive skin and those dessert-worthy caramel eyes.

Ellery had donned a vintage T-shirt, shorts and leather flip-flops. The outfit was simple, casual. She'd purposely not put much thought into it because she'd been trying to prove to herself that she wasn't into Behr like *that*. But seeing him made her regret not adding a hint more makeup, not styling her hair instead of pulling it into two low, short pigtails.

Stop right now! Behr is otherwise occupied, as he's told you many times. And for all Ellery knew, Behr didn't even find her attractive. She was the one drooling over him.

"Hey." He flicked one pigtail. "You look cute with your hair like that." If only he didn't say it so casually. The unaffected delivery really negated it being taken at anything more than face value.

"Thanks." She, too, could manage effortless and breezy and no big deal. Or at least she'd managed to this time.

"Margo." Behr nodded at the dog as if she were an acquaintance at a party whom he'd rather avoid.

"Let's walk a bit before Brynn gets here. I thought we could do the path around the park."

"Walking I'll agree to. Your plan I'm still not sure about."

"Noted." Ellery handed Behr the leash and they took to the trail. It pained her to push Behr, and yet she had to a little or this would never happen. Ellery had spoken to Kapp at length, God bless him for giving his time, and he'd agreed that with Behr doing well and making progress, an experience in public was smart. And an experience practicing how to deflect and have Margo block if another dog approached was even better. Which was why she'd recruited Brynn and her Yorkshire Terrier mix, Woodrow, who looked very much like a stuffed-animal toy dog with his soft fluffy hair and his bow tie collar covered in dinosaurs. Surely Woodrow's small size would put Behr at ease. Ellery hoped so, because training with a dog that didn't terrorize Behr would be a plus.

"I have a treat for you if you can get through this. Margo is always getting treats during training. I thought maybe you needed some motivation, too, to make it through this session."

Behr's scowl fell away. "What is it?"

"I'm not telling. You'll have to be surprised."

"I think I'd do a better job if I knew what my reward was."

"You're seriously ten years old."

"I like to think of myself as a little more mature than that. More like twelve."

Ellery laughed.

The birds and the squirrels were busy this evening, but Margo was focused and on point exactly as she should be.

She held her head high, checking on Behr every few seconds like he was her prize to protect. It was almost as if she'd been patiently waiting for Behr to be ready, for Behr to trust her.

And it would be just like sensitive Margo to recognize that this day was big. They were training outside. They could encounter any number of things at the park—people or animals. Ellery's stomach filled with dragonfly wings. Whatever happened, God was with them. Behr's family had assured her they were also praying for his training with Margo, and that gave her added peace.

"Seems like Fletcher is doing okay with the ankle this week." Behr inhaled, exhaled, then gripped the harness tighter, his knuckles turning white. "I haven't heard any complaints from him, and he's been doing all of the activities at MENtor camp."

"Good. He didn't mention sitting out from anything, though who knows if he would tell me if that were the case." He'd spent the weekend icing his ankle and elevating it like Alessandra had instructed him to, and by Monday, he'd been back at camp. Ellery had been surprised he didn't use the slight injury as an excuse to miss. She wasn't sure if it was the promise of a dog that kept him going or little changes like Behr had said. Either way, she considered it a relief that he was back in the saddle.

"Did I tell you that I think I found a dog for Fletch?" At Behr's quick head shake, Ellery continued. "One of our service dog trainers has been working with a German shorthaired pointer, but he's a counter surfer and they can't get him to break the habit. Which means he's not the right fit for the program. Which means he could be a good fit for Fletcher. Although, he requires a lot of exercise. Desiree will probably kill me for gifting her son with a hyperactive dog who likes to steal food."

"The dog sounds like the canine version of a feisty teenager. Fitting."

"I thought the *exact* same thing." And Ellery was way too entertained by that.

Across the park, Brynn pulled up. When she opened the backdoor to let Woodrow out, Behr's response was a sigh big enough to rustle leaves.

"The other option is for you to run into another dog while you're out with Margo and not have your plan down. This way you won't even have to think. You'll just do, and so will Margo."

"If you say so, kid." Behr checked his phone as Brynn and Woodrow headed in their direction. "Twenty-two minutes left on the clock."

"Stinker."

"What?" He played the innocence card like a pro. "I'm just following Kapp's advice."

Right. And Ellery was just controlled enough not to find Behr's playfulness endearing.

* * *

Brynn and her little runt dog stopped about ten feet from Behr and Ellery. He appreciated the space she was giving him.

"Hi, Hot Veteran."

Hot veteran. Huh. His mood shot from stressed to intrigued.

He faced Ellery. "Been talking about me, have you?"

"Nope. Brynn snooped you online. Any opinions are hers alone."

Oh. That wasn't nearly as fun, then. But if Ellery's friend had that opinion of him, maybe the roots of it had come from Ellery. Behr resisted a headshake and an eye roll and every other what-are-you-thinking response that his reaction deserved. His dad's encouragement or advice or whatever that had been the other night had really messed with him.

"This is my friend Brynn and her dog, Woodrow."

Behr nodded in greeting. "Appreciate you coming to torture me."

"Anytime." Brynn broke into a smile that said, *Torture is my middle name,* and Behr broke into a sweat. "So what's our plan, Elle?" she asked, turning to Ellery.

"Behr's going to work on having Margo block when you approach. We've already practiced it, but I want the two of them to get the habit down in a live scenario."

"Cool. So should we just run at you or—"

"No!" Behr and Ellery responded at the same time.

Brynn's laughter was far too delighted. This woman was a little scary.

"Like I would ever."

"You've got jokes, huh." Behr's pulse exchanged its manic jump roping for the consistency of a light rain. "I can't really judge you for that since I'm typically the same way."

"I don't know about that. Ellery says you're not that funny, to be honest."

Ellery hooted. Woodrow yipped. Behr cracked up. Margo looked at all of them like they were from another planet.

"I would say we're going to get along just fine." And why would Behr expect any less from a friend of Ellery's? She picked good people. She'd decided pretty quickly to be his friend, hadn't she? He might be broken and damaged, but his heart was still in working condition. For the most part.

"You ready?" Ellery asked him, using that tender tone that said she cared deeply about his answer. The one that reminded him of his mom touching his dad's arm.

She should really stop talking to Behr like that.

He also *really* didn't want her to.

"Will saying no end this little experiment?" Behr gripped Margo's harness like she was his lifeline, his saving grace, his ride-or-die. How ironic.

"It's not an experiment. It's practice. There's a difference."

He disagreed, but what choice did he have? She was right that he needed to be prepared for public outings. "Fine. Let the torture begin."

"You'll do great! You've done this before." Minus the other dog. Ellery's response to Behr's cynicism was perky and infused with cheer. Her nonverbals were shouting *You can do this!*

His nonverbals didn't want to be here, even if his trainer was the main draw for his presence.

"Okay. You remember the block is when Margo is behind, and cover is when she's in front, right?"

"Right."

"A dog could come from any direction, so you'll definitely need both."

"Not helping anything."

Ellery's look said she was partially amused by him and entirely sympathetic. She could fit a lot into one expression on that pretty face of hers. And he could fit a lot of distraction into five seconds of training.

"It's not just about her creating a barrier between you and another dog. A lot of veterans like their service dog behind them in a store, protecting their back." That made sense. Behr definitely had to curb the desire to be hyperalert. "Brynn, head our way. Behr, take the hand you're using for target and swipe it across your body like we did the other day."

He slid his hand across his abdomen, but Margo stayed put, tail wagging, her attention bouncing between Behr, Ellery, Brynn and Woodrow. If Margo wanted to, she could pick little Woodrow up in her jaws and cart him around like a chew toy. But Margo would never do that. She was far too chill. Behr was the one with zero chill.

Especially after the way his phone call with Marina had ended earlier this morning. He'd FaceTimed with her and the kids, and their excitement over seeing him at the end of next week had turned his trajectory back toward them. The three of them were his mission. They needed his attention more than anyone else did—including himself. But after the kids had run off to play, Marina had said she had something to tell him. Something important. Behr hadn't been able to pinpoint if she'd sounded excited, upset or somewhere in between.

Tell me now, he'd responded. Good or bad, he'd rather know what it was.

But Marina had said it was the kind of thing that had to be done—said—in person. What did *that* mean?

"Did you hear me?" Instead of snapping at him like he deserved, Ellery's question was even-tempered, with a dash of curiosity.

"Sorry. No. I'm…something is on my mind. I'll turn it off. Promise."

"Can you really do that?"

"I'm usually good at compartmentalizing. I don't know what's wrong with me today."

"Two dogs?"

She read him like Behr's ancient next-door neighbor did the weekday paper. "Maybe. Let's keep going."

"Are you sure?"

"Yep." Brynn was here just to help him. Behr wasn't going to waste her time.

"Here." Ellery grabbed his hand and stood directly in front of him, her back to his chest. "Brynn, head our way." Behr had practiced this before, so he shouldn't need Ellery's assistance. But her close proximity glued his jaw shut. He could stay here, minus the dogs, for the next few hours. Ellery smelled citrusy and fresh, and he wanted to tug on one of her pigtails again like an elementary kid pretending he didn't have a crush.

Only she could make pigtails adorable and alluring.

Woodrow, oblivious as to what they were up to, trotted along with Brynn.

When they neared, Ellery moved their joined hands across her abdomen. Margo instantly created the cover.

"Why does she follow you and not me? What am I doing wrong?"

"Be confident. All Margo wants to do is please you. Be strong with her so she knows how."

Strong. How could he do that when this situation made him weak on top of weak on top of weak?

Despite their conversation, Ellery hadn't moved. She was still standing close enough that they could be considered one person if you squinted, which was exactly what Brynn was doing. Her expression said, *I've got your number. I know more of what's going on between you two than you do.* She should hang with his sisters. They owned that same mug.

Behr shoved aside any guilt about being so close to Ellery. This wasn't a romantic thing. This was a necessary thing. And if he wanted training to work, he had to concentrate on Margo. Not on the woman who was tucked against him like wrapping paper on a gift box.

"Let's do it one more time." Ellery squeezed

his hand in encouragement, and Behr barely resisted entwining their fingers. Woodrow and Brynn walked their way. Ellery and Behr's joint motion was fluid. Margo moved into position. Behr's hand heated and then went clammy at Ellery's touch. What in the world? Was he fifteen with his first crush? His adrenaline had to be about the dogs and the training, not the woman. Had to be.

Once Woodrow reached Margo, he wanted to say hello with a round of intrusive sniffing, but Margo didn't even feign interest. Good girl. Now if only Behr could follow suit with Ellery. He was a mess today, thoughts bouncing from Ellery to Marina. If something was wrong, Marina would have told him over the phone, right? She wouldn't make him wait. It had to be good news, didn't it?

Ellery stepped away and faced him. "That was great. Let's try it again with just you this time."

Brynn backed up. Woodrow had to be wondering why they were traversing the same patch of sidewalk over and over again, but the dog found something new to distract him each time. He made Margo look like the queen of concentration. Behr was only handling Woodrow's presence because Brynn was keeping him away between attempts. Despite the tough persona she'd displayed when she got here, Brynn was as careful with him as Ellery was. Behr should be embarrassed they had to baby him, but he was just grateful to be dealing with only one canine adjustment at a time.

When Brynn and Woodrow neared, Behr gave the signal. Margo took her position. The world stopped turning.

Ellery broke into a cheer, her hands flying into the air like a flyer celebrating a competition victory. His sister Suzette had been on a competitive squad, and Behr was firmly on the cheer-was-a-sport side of the argument. Suzette's squad had done some impressive stuff that most of the soldiers he knew—including himself—could never attempt.

Brynn's brows shot up along with the corners of her mouth. "Well done, HV."

"Thanks." He laughed at the nickname, not sure a simple win deserved this much fanfare.

The snap of a car door closing made all of them—even the dogs—glance across the park. A woman had gotten out of her car and was moving around to the back hatch of the vehicle.

Ellery tensed first since she was the first one to realize what was happening. Behr caught on quickly. The woman was letting her dog out of the back. Of course Ellery was concerned about him, but he would be fine. He'd just learned what to do if the new canine arrival were to approach him, and the woman would likely just be walking the perimeter of the park anyway with her dog. It was time to put on his big boy britches and handle it, just like he'd have to in the real world...when Ellery abandoned him to manage Margo on his own.

Cue panic.

I'll be fine. I'm not in this battle alone, remember?

And if that mantra didn't fully put him at peace yet, surely it would. Someday.

Chapter Thirteen

Behr's pathetic pep talk unraveled as quickly as the scene before him.

Once the woman opened the hatch, her dog jumped out—unleashed. It was a pit bull. People often said pit bulls got a bad rap. And Behr was happy to believe them on that as long as he was on the other side of the fence from one. Or behind plexiglass. Inside an armored tank.

But before he had time to panic over the loose dog, two more canines—mixed breeds—leaped from the vehicle. Also unleashed.

"Three." That was all he could get out. All he could utter. He'd been planning to use his mantra as a crutch, but *battle*, *alone* and *nope* were the only fragmented thoughts currently rattling around in his brain.

The dogs bounded into the grassy center of

the park, noticed their group and then switched tacks, traveling in their direction at a swift pace.

Brynn scooped up Woodrow. Behr was pretty sure the growl that followed came from Ellery, not Margo.

Margo was blocking the dogs' approach, but Behr couldn't imagine that would be enough to stop the trio. Especially not when the woman who owned them was sauntering behind, clueless as to the escalating panic her arrival had created.

The pack split and rounded them like they were planning to approach from the back side. Behr should move Margo to cover. Or block. He couldn't remember which was which right now. But he was incapable of that because his arm had gone limp—useless—the limb unable to compute the message his brain was screeching.

Right when Behr thought he might melt into the ground, Ellery morphed into a superhero.

"Stop!" She raised her hands and bellowed the command at the dogs.

The pit bull swung left and then right but didn't continue forward, the second dog stopped in its tracks, and the third plopped its behind right down on the ground like it had never been reprimanded before.

"Behr. Take Margo and get in my vehicle, please. It's open." Ellery's instructions were calm but dripping with white-hot fury. Behr almost felt sorry for the owner of the dogs, who was now approaching. Almost but not quite.

He did as Ellery had directed. Brynn, too, escaped. They both gave a clipped wave to each other as they made their way to the vehicles. Behr would thank Brynn later for her time and for putting up with him.

He loaded Margo in the back seat and then climbed into the passenger side of Ellery's truck, willing his sporadic pulse to even out. His head was floating like a helium balloon at the end of a long string.

A nose landed on his shoulder and a puff of dog breath fanned his cheek. Behr had been avoiding face-to-face contact with Margo because he wasn't sure how he would react. And he'd imagined *not good* was high on the probability list. But the pressure of her steady chin on his shoulder…instead of sending him straight into a wall of panic, stabilized his anxieties.

I can do this with God's help. I'm not alone in this battle.

Not only did Behr have God on his side, he had Ellery to back him up. If it was wrong to cower behind a girl when a dog came his way, then Behr didn't want to be right.

He lifted a hand, settling it on Margo's head.

She nuzzled closer. Like she was sending a message that he could trust her.

He was working on it with every ounce of himself. "Ellery is going to freak out that I'm not completely freaking out right now." Especially after his adrenaline spike.

Only God could have orchestrated this moment and Behr's reaction. All those prayers going up about his training with Margo must be working.

He heard yelling and focused his attention on the park. Speaking of freaking out. Even through the vehicle he could catch most of Ellery's tirade.

"Can't have dogs unleashed...public park."

Based on her body language, the woman was responding in a defensive, heated manner, though Behr couldn't catch her words.

"Everyone should follow the rules!" Ellery, on the other hand, was loud enough that someone in the next town could hear. "You have no idea what you've just done!"

The woman began backing away. Ellery must have lowered her voice, because Behr could no longer catch her words, just the delivery. Lots of animated gestures and upper-body action going on with his girl.

His girl.

Insert the grimace emoji times ten. Behr

hadn't meant that. Or at least he hadn't meant to think it.

The woman corralled her dogs over to her vehicle, and Ellery stomped toward the truck. She ripped open the driver's door and hopped inside, slamming it behind her.

"What is wrong with people!" Her fierce, sparking green eyes swung to him. "Are you okay? I mean I know you're not, but are you?"

"Little shaky but I'm all right." Despite the situation, his mouth eased into the start of a smile. "Are *you* okay? Seemed a little...feisty out there."

"Not really. That made me so angry. She has no idea how far that interaction could have set you back. And there are signs posted on both sides of the park that dogs need to be leashed. I made sure of that this weekend."

She'd driven over here to scout the park? Behr's heart began pinging like a metal detector homing in on a prize.

"Not gonna lie—seeing you go Incredible Hulk like that might be the highlight of my year. Way scarier than when you knocked down my door. You've been saving up."

Her cheeks creased begrudgingly. "I was defending you!"

"I know. I liked it. I imagine she'll never come back to this park again."

"And she shouldn't! Unless her dogs are leashed!"

Amusement vibrated in his chest. He was mesmerized by this version of Ellery with her scarlet cheeks, her reaction as fiery as metal meeting the road at one hundred miles per hour.

Behr chose to find humor in the moment, because if he didn't, he was going to unearth something else—attraction that had been simmering beneath the surface ever since he'd first met Ellery. Attraction that, in the aftermath of Dad's quiet commentary, Behr had begun to fear was *more*. More than he'd bargained for. More than he'd allowed himself to admit.

And that direction was off-limits for him. He was committed elsewhere, at least for the time being. At least until Marina got through this hard stage with the kids.

But if Behr wasn't otherwise involved, he'd tell Ellery just how much he appreciated her fighting for him in all the ways she already had *and* the altercation she'd just won with flying colors.

Not that he was judging the fight or anything.

But if he were to, Ellery would win hands down. Everything including his heart.

Ellery had done her best to empathize with Behr's fear of dogs. She'd prided herself on understanding at least where he was coming from. But the white-hot anxiety he must feel on the daily had eluded her—until about five minutes ago.

When she'd realized that the woman was releasing unleashed dogs from her vehicle, Ellery had internally imploded. And then once Behr was safely in her truck, externally exploded.

She felt the tiniest bit of remorse for yelling at the woman—she could have handled that part better—but she didn't regret anything she'd said. It was all true. The woman *should* have had her dogs leashed. She *should* know better than to take them out in public when she had no real control over their actions.

Margo, on the other hand, had behaved perfectly even under pressure and stress. "When I was walking over to the truck—"

"*Walking* is a bit lenient, wouldn't you say? I'd go with *stomping, storming, angry speed-walking*—"

"Point taken," Ellery interrupted dryly. She wasn't finding all of this quite as amusing as Behr seemed to be. She'd expected him to be in the fetal position when she'd reached the vehicle. But she was almost certain that Margo had been majorly invading the front seat...and Behr had been calm. "Was Margo in the front seat with you when I got over here?"

"Not exactly, but her chin was on my shoulder."

Not words she'd ever expected to hear from Behr. At least not without accompanying panic.

"Did you...how did that go?"

"Better than I would have expected it to. I think she was comforting me, and I'd say it worked."

"Well. That's about the best news ever."

"Thought that might be your response."

"Isn't it yours?"

"For the most part. I wouldn't say I'm perfectly healed or anything."

"But it's a big improvement."

He paused and then answered slowly, as if admitting it not only to her, but to himself. "It's a big improvement."

Ellery barely resisted hopping out of the truck to do a happy dance. Thankfully, the woman with the dogs had left immediately. Another ping of regret at the way Ellery had responded to her surfaced. But she hadn't been rational in that moment. She'd been irate thinking of the woman's irresponsibility.

That encounter could have completely derailed Behr, and it was absolutely astounding that it hadn't.

"I can see the anger resurfacing." Behr motioned to her face.

"Who *does* that? And shows no remorse? It could have been so much worse. If one of them had gotten too close to you or nipped at you…"

"We'd be back to way before square one."

"Exactly."

"Then thank God that didn't happen. Based on how things have been improving with how I feel around Margo and the help from Kapp, I'd say God certainly has His hand in this. In how things have been progressing."

"Amen to that." And since Behr was doing so well… "I think when you take the boys camping on Friday night, Margo should go with you."

Behr choked on absolutely nothing. He hacked, his pupils wide and sporting the panic Ellery had expected when she'd reached her vehicle. The whole episode caused Margo to sit up and study him like a wary, concerned mother.

When he finally quit, she dropped her chin back to her paws on the back seat.

"Don't you think that's moving too fast? I can barely touch her."

"You've been petting her each time. She just touched you and you handled it."

"There's a whole lot of difference between handling something for a few seconds or even thirty minutes versus camping overnight with a group of teens. That just sounds like a recipe for disaster."

"Will you guys be hiking?"

Behr's jaw twitched. He stared straight out the windshield. "Didn't you say you had a treat lined up for me tonight?"

Margo's head popped between their seats.

"He's not talking to you. Sorry, Margo-girl. I did. I do, I guess. If you're still up for it. And you didn't answer my question."

"Show me the…*thing.*" He'd avoided saying *treat* again, but Margo was still listening to their every word, still nosing into their conversation. "And I'll answer your question."

"Preteen."

"Taskmaster."

"Fine." Ellery wasn't going to win this conversation. At least not until Behr had his treat. "Why don't you just ride with me and then I'll drop you back here after."

Behr rubbed his palms together. "Done."

Ellery drove until she hit a dirt road and then continued on for a couple miles. She slowed where there was a small turnoff. Barely enough for two or three cars to edge in close together, though no one else was currently there.

She pulled over and parked. "Why don't you practice getting Margo out and I'll grab the stuff from the truck bed."

"All right." Behr opened the back door,

grabbed Margo's leash and directed her to jump out. Once she did, she stood by his left side, waiting for further direction. She was so good she almost made him capable. Almost. But camping? Ellery was pushing too hard with that one. It would take everything Behr had in him to keep up with those boys and the other chaperones for the night and for his body to handle sleeping on the ground. But he was determined to do it. Somehow. Because it felt like a slice of normal, and Behr was fighting for as much of that as he could get.

Ellery removed a small white box and paper bag from the bed of the truck. She motioned for Behr to follow her, so he and Margo did. She walked on an uneven trail, and Behr moved his grip from Margo's leash to the harness she was still wearing.

Should he have taken that off her in the truck? He'd been so intent on escaping an altercation with the dogs he'd completely forgotten about it. If he was going to care for Margo, he had better learn the ins and outs. He'd ask Ellery whether the harness needed to be removed in transit or not.

The trail led to a clearing and a rocky ledge, and below, Mt. Vista Lake was small but sparkling.

Ellery dropped to a seated position. Behr

joined her. He directed Margo to lie beside him, which she did.

"Well done."

He scooted forward until his legs dangled over the edge of the cliff.

Ellery wheezed. "What are you doing? Scoot back!"

"I'm not going to go over the edge."

"But what if you do?"

Translated: but what if your balance tricks you and you plummet to your death?

Irritation seeped from his chest, and he inched back. It was less comfortable to sit this way, plus he felt like his mom and sisters were here directing him.

"That better?"

"Yes. If something happened to you after all that's happened to you, your family would never forgive me."

"Unless you're giving me a shove off the cliff, I don't know how me falling would have anything to do with you."

Her eyelids squeezed shut. "Thank you for that terrible, terrible image."

"Wait—so you're saying you'd miss me if something happened to me?" Her eyes popped open in time to roll, and Behr chuckled. "So, what did you bring me? Or is this the *thing*?" He nodded to the view.

"This isn't the thing, though it could be." Ellery scanned the mix of aspen and evergreen trees surrounding the turquoise water. "This is my favorite place. I come here to think or pray or just be."

And she was letting him crash her place. Behr understood the value of that with Ellery. She gave a lot to other people. For her to share her spot with him meant he must be safe, too. And that might be the best realization he'd had in years. The tap-tap-tap in his chest ramped up.

"Thanks for letting me tag along."

"Anytime." The word carried weight. Like she meant it. Again, Behr's heart fired like an M2 machine gun.

"Here, Margo." She retrieved a bone from the bag and tossed it to the dog, who began chewing it contentedly.

Ellery opened the white box and placed it between them. A pie was nestled inside.

"Strawberry rhubarb?" He'd mentioned his favorite dessert to Ellery one time. It was so *her* to remember.

"Yep. I thought we needed to celebrate how far you've come with Margo. Do you realize she's chewing that bone right next to you?"

"Oh, I know she's chewing the bone. I am aware of everything she does. Just because I'm handling it doesn't mean it's necessarily easy."

Her face morphed with concern. "But you're doing okay at the moment?"

"Yeah. Especially if that pie comes with a fork."

She removed paper plates from the bag and two forks, along with a plastic pie server. The edge of it was serrated, so she sliced the pie and scooped a piece onto his plate. Behr didn't even wait for Ellery to dish her own before digging in.

"Is this still warm? Fresh?" He spoke around the food he'd just shoveled into his mouth like the ten-year-old Ellery claimed he was.

"I picked the pie up fresh on the way to the park. Karen Anelia, who is the opposite of the way people use the name Karen now, like every other wonderful Karen I know, bakes from home and sells locally. She supplies a few of the restaurants in town."

The pie deserved one thousand awards. Karen was his new favorite word.

"This is the best strawberry rhubarb I've ever tasted." He finished the piece before Ellery had taken two bites of hers. "Can I have seconds?"

She handed him the pie server. He should take a small piece the second time. But he didn't.

He downed another bite, the tart and sweet combination melting on his tongue. "When I was deployed and came home, this was always my first request."

"What did you miss the most?"

"Probably my family. But don't you dare tell them that."

Ellery smiled, still savoring her first piece. "I'm not sure what happened to my family or where we went wrong. Maybe it hurts my parents too much to be close after losing Ace. But your family…" Her gaze flickered to him. "I can see how you'd miss them. They're pretty amazing."

"And by amazing you mean nosy and intrusive."

Her laughter burrowed into his chest, as warm and appealing as the pie. "Is your trip to see Marina and the kids still on for the end of next week?"

He nodded since his mouth was full.

Ellery scraped the last bite from her plate. "Did you and Marina ever consider… I know you're not there now, but did you ever entertain the idea of dating each other?"

Behr swallowed. He didn't get into this with very many people. But then, Ellery wasn't just anyone. She'd quickly moved into the top three contacts he used on his phone.

"When the women in my family kept pushing and hinting at that, I contemplated it. Tried to process that concept. It never clicked for me. It was too weird. For me *and* Marina, I think. I knew her too well as Jake's wife. She'll always be that in my mind."

"That makes sense. And it's good your sisters are so understanding of that."

He laughed.

"Are you ready to talk about taking Margo camping yet? You never answered if there would be hiking."

Behr passed Ellery his plate so that she could toss it into the bag with hers. Margo was still intrigued by her bone, her body laid out next to Behr. He was beginning to believe that if he needed her or her assistance, she'd understand that and jump to action in a millisecond.

He was drinking Ellery's Kool-Aid of hope. But he also still felt weak. Shaky. Like a newborn.

"I don't want to admit there will be a small amount of hiking, because then you'll say that Margo should go with me because the ground will be uneven."

"Did you use her support getting to this spot?" Ellery's focus was on him, her expression brimming with hope and questions and more hope.

Behr forced out an answer. "I did."

She didn't respond right away. She was like a

mom teaching a lesson and waiting for her kid to get the point. Was it any wonder teenagers were so annoyed by their parents?

"I know where you're going with this, but I still don't think it's a good idea. What if things backfire while I'm helping to lead a group of teen boys? It's too much pressure." He hated his inability so much at this moment. "I can't do it. I'm sorry."

"*I'm* sorry. You've come a long way, Behr. And I'm not saying that because I'm trying to convince you to take Margo when you go camping. If that doesn't happen, then it doesn't happen. Tonight at the park was traumatic. If you were alone in a store with Margo and a dog came by, it would be one dog. Leashed. Tonight was like the perfect storm. The worst-case scenario. But you did survive it. You handled it. Let's just focus on that for now."

He hadn't handled it. Ellery had. "The only reason I did okay at the park was because you were there, stopping the dogs from fully approaching."

"If I hadn't been there, you would have removed yourself from the situation. You would have left immediately."

"We tried! The dogs moved so fast—and their owner so slow—I couldn't have. No, I definitely wouldn't have weathered that storm without you. That's why the idea of taking Margo camping is debilitating." Admitting all of this was hard for him, but Behr pushed on. Kapp had encouraged him to be honest. He'd said that openness would bring healing. "The fear of dogs that developed during deployment, the fear now, the fear tonight—it all blends together. I'm not denying that things are improving with Margo. But it's all…it's all still there."

"The park was an extreme situation," Ellery said quietly. "I shouldn't have pushed you about camping right away after."

Behr reached over, squeezed her arm. "Stop." His thumb etched a path across her soft skin. "You didn't do anything wrong. It's just—my whole life I've felt capable. Strong. But this new janky version of my brain makes me feel like every battle is a loss."

The sound of Margo's chewing filled the silence. "Sometimes surviving something, handling something like tonight, even if it doesn't go perfectly, *is* winning."

In theory Behr could agree. But when it came to himself…that was a flavor of Kool-Aid he wasn't ready to drink yet.

Chapter Fourteen

"**Y**ou're in a mood." Fletcher's comment to Behr was comical since everything Fletcher did was a mood.

The teen stood just inside Behr's office, ready for his ride home. The ride Behr had been avoiding because it would bring him face-to-face with Ellery. At which time she would confirm plans for him to take Margo on the camping trip tomorrow night, despite his many protests about that very thing.

"I just have a lot on my mind." He'd had a productive training session with Margo yesterday after work and that had pushed him off the cliff that he and Ellery had been on after the Tuesday evening park fiasco. She'd gone from hoping he would take Margo on the camping trip to expecting him to. She'd been all soft and kind and Ellery about it. Not nearly as pushy as one of his sisters would be, but still, Behr felt sick considering it. He wasn't strong enough. Brave enough. The mental struggle was like fighting an invisible enemy. He much preferred physical combat.

"Give me the good, the bad and the I-could-live-without." Fletcher was obviously relishing the opportunity to turn the question back on Behr.

The kid probably didn't expect Behr to level with him, so he decided to do exactly that. "Your aunt wants me to take Margo camping with us tomorrow."

Fletcher shrugged as if to say, *So? Why does that matter? Isn't that what you were going for as an end result?*

"In case you haven't realized why Ellery is working so hard to train me individually with Margo, it's because I have some kind of... trauma or fear or whatever you want to call it about dogs. I had a few encounters on various tours, and it messed me up."

There. He'd laid it out. Maybe now Fletcher would understand. Would Behr ever be able to take Margo home? It felt impossible. So, like Fletcher had implied with that shrug, why had Behr gone through all of the training?

"Margo freaks you out, but you've been training with her anyway?"

"Yep."

"Huh. That's impressive."

Wait—what? Was that a compliment coming from teenzilla?

"If you lose it or something goes wrong with Margo while we're camping, I can step in. I'll be there the whole time."

Behr's chair rolled away from his desk like an aftershock to an explosion. He didn't respond. Couldn't form words.

"I mean, would that help? If you knew you had backup? If you have an issue with her, just give me a signal and I'll take her for a bit." Backup was one of the things they taught at MENtor camp. They coached the boys to ask for it when they needed it and to provide it when others did. Behr wondered if Fletcher even realized what he was saying or the roots of it. But he certainly wasn't going to ruin the moment by bringing that up.

Behr cleared emotion and surprise and gratitude from his throat. "Yeah. That would help. A lot." But it would also mean he had to follow through and take Margo. Because now he didn't have any excuse not to. "Are you sure you're good with that?"

"Sure. I like Margo. I'm in charge of her while she's staying on-site. She's one of my favorite things about being here. And Ellery's been having me go through various training exercises with her, too. Not sure if she's training me or the dog." His mouth lifted along with his shoulders.

"Do you—would you consider training dogs for Helping Paws in the future?" The idea that Fletcher might step into a role like that because of his time with Ellery was huge.

"Yeah. I would. It seems like a way to be close to my dad even though I can't be close to him. If that makes any sense."

"That makes a ton of sense."

Fletcher accepted Behr's encouragement with a nod. "I'll meet you at the car." Fletcher stepped into the hallway, his exit signaling that the conversation was done. As if he was all talked out. Had shared enough. And he had. Behr was frankly shocked by the dialogue that had just transpired. And by the results of it… which left him no choice but to say yes to taking Margo on the camping trip—and to facing his debilitating fear. All with a crowd of boys and co-chaperones to watch.

"Did I do the right thing?" Ellery pressed the speaker button and set the phone on the counter so she could make chicken salad while talking to Brynn. She had to keep herself busy, and

Fletcher would likely be hungry when he got home from the camping trip. Behr, too.

That question had been bearing down on Ellery since she'd woken at 4 a.m. She was the one who'd pushed Behr to take Margo on this trip, though Kapp had agreed and supported the plan.

She'd meant well. Margo would be helpful to Behr on the uneven terrain he might encounter while with a bunch of capable-bodied boys who could bounce back like cats falling and landing on all four paws. But Behr's system didn't work like that anymore. Which was why she'd been so adamant that Margo accompany him. But now Ellery was second-guessing. Maybe Behr should have attempted to take Margo home by himself first. Though he had said knowing he had Fletcher's support had calmed him. And with a big group, Behr could pawn Margo off on any of the boys or other leaders at any time and get a few minutes to himself to regroup.

See? He'd be fine.

"You did the right thing. Things will work out even if Behr has to ask for help. Isn't that part of life? They probably teach that at MENtor camp."

"They probably do." Ellery heard a vehicle outside and dropped the knife. It clattered onto the counter. "I think they're here!"

"Let me know how it went when you can."

They disconnected and Ellery moved slowly to the front door in order not to display the nervous excitement she was feeling on the inside.

When she reached the front step, Fletcher was on the bottom one. Without argument, he hugged her hello. Her heart went squishy. She'd missed him. Missed the grunts and eye rolls and his begrudging smile that always felt like a win.

"Need a shower." He continued inside the house.

"Wait! At least tell me how it went."

"Good. I'll fill you in after." The front door swung shut behind him.

Behr had gotten out of his vehicle and was opening the back door to let Margo out. Ellery approached with her hands in the praying position in front of her chest.

"How was it?" She went up on her tiptoes as she waited for him to turn and answer.

He faced her as Margo stood on his left side. Good girl. Always on duty.

"Backfired big time."

Ellery's stomach bottomed out. "Oh no." She blinked rapidly to clear the rush of moisture. What had gone wrong?

"Are you tearing up? Stop it right now." He pulled her into an unexpected hug. "I'm teasing. It went great. Margo was a champ." His arms tightened around her, and Ellery tucked against his chest like a kid giving in to a nap after a long fight. "Margo was helpful just like you'd said she would be."

Buried against the brick wall that was Behr, Ellery inhaled the scent of him mixed with evergreen and outdoors. "That was the worst joke ever. You're a terrible person."

His chest shook with quiet laughter. "I'm sorry. I thought you'd be able to read me."

She should be able to, shouldn't she? Like this hug, for example…what did *it* mean? Because it was lingering past the allotted amount of time for a friend and quickly sliding into holding each other. Admitting they'd missed each other. Admitting that things between them were progressing beyond those boundaries they'd first set in place.

Behr let go, and Ellery reluctantly stepped back from him. Maybe those thoughts tumbling around in her brain like whites on a hot cycle were all her. Maybe Behr didn't share them. He'd certainly been clear with her from the start that his attention and support were otherwise occupied.

"I need details. I've been dying waiting for you guys to get back."

"Fletcher did great. He had a good time as far as I could tell. And I noticed he's made a few friends. I found out last night that two don't live far from him in Denver. They were already making plans to get together when Fletcher returns to his mom's."

"That's fabulous. Desiree will be ecstatic." The helium balloon reserved for Fletcher inside Ellery released a long puff.

"And what about you and Margo?" Ellery asked. "Seriously this time."

His mouth bowed at her inquisition, and she did her best to keep her attention elsewhere. On his caramel eyes. The extra stubble lining his cheeks and chin. The way his hair looked like it hadn't been touched since he'd mashed one side of it sleeping. Well. Those distractions weren't helping anything.

"I did great with Margo. There was some uneven terrain, and she was perfect. Only had one moment of concern with sleeping arrangements. I wasn't sure where to position her so that she wasn't by my face when I woke up. Was afraid I might panic in that situation. But then—" his Adam's apple bobbed "—Fletcher appeared. He slept next to me and had Margo stick close to him. One glance and Fletcher knew I needed the rescue."

"Fletch." This time the moisture clogged her throat. "That's the best news I've heard in ages. Desiree is going to weep when I relay it." Ellery paused. Would Behr want her sharing that, though? "I mean, if it's okay that I tell her."

"Of course. I want her to know how great he's doing." How did Behr not realize that his vulnerability and willingness to share something like that with Desiree was incredibly strong? And, Ellery had to admit, it only added to the attraction she felt for him.

"Do you want to come in? I'm mixing up chicken salad for sandwiches. Thought you two might be hungry."

Behr's vision tracked over her shoulder to the house. Ellery's breath stalled. She'd missed Fletcher, yes, but she'd also missed Behr. And he'd only been gone one night. She was a little concerned that noticing Behr's absence so acutely was a deterrent on the road to Helping Paws' success. She'd definitely developed deeper feelings for him than she'd planned to allow herself.

"I really should head home. I need a shower."

Ellery's disappointment registered at losing-a-pet levels. "Right. Of course. You'll probably need to rest today, too. I'm sure last night wasn't the best sleep."

"True. Don't want to push my body too hard so that it breaks down. Again." Behr held out Margo's leash. Ellery stared at it, confused. "Aren't you going to take her? Or do you want

Fletcher to do it? He mentioned you've been having him work with Margo some."

"Behr." Ellery wasn't sure how to break this news to him. "I'm not taking Margo back. You made it through the night. Take her home. She's yours."

The *she's yours* registered on Behr's face with total and complete shock. Had he really expected to do well with Margo and then return her? The whole point was for Behr to have the assistance he needed. If his fears had dissipated enough or were at least manageable enough that he could handle Margo now, why wouldn't he take her home?

He raked a hand through his hair. "This was your plan all along, wasn't it?"

That made her sound diabolical. "I assumed it was your plan, too."

"I hadn't thought beyond surviving the night. I feel like Fletcher when his mom came to talk to him about potentially moving."

She'd completely blindsided him? "I mean, it's not like Margo can't stay here." Ellery was caving to his fears, and it was unnecessary. Behr would be fine. She had complete confidence in Margo, Behr and God. "But I know you can do this. I have absolute faith that you're ready to take Margo home, Behr. Kapp agreed that if last night went well, it was time. I guess I—we—should have relayed that to you."

"Kapp did mention something like that during our last session," Behr admitted begrudgingly. "But I put it out of my mind. I guess I assumed something wouldn't go well on the camping trip. I thought it might set me back."

"But it didn't. You're strong. I know you like to think otherwise, but it's not true."

"I had to have Margo sleep by Fletcher!" The corded muscles in his arms popped, and his forehead erupted in worry lines. His agitation made Ellery want to step forward and reengage in that embrace. It killed her to see Behr struggle like this. "What if I take her home and freak out and there's no Fletcher to save me? What if I panic in the middle of the night because I wake up and there's a dog staring me down? It's not like I haven't dreamed about a dog attacking me before. How will that nightmare *not* be resurrected if I take her home?" His fingertips dug into his temple. "I hate this."

And Ellery hated it for him. "If you need me, I'm a text or phone call away. Any time of night." She wanted to fix this with everything in her. Offer to sleep on Behr's couch. Offer to keep Margo. But if he didn't rip off the Band-Aid and do this, when would it ever be the right time?

It wasn't helping that she'd grown these

crushing feelings for Behr. That she cared about him as more than a friend. That only made her want to rescue him more. But she feared the best way to do that was to let him figure it out with Margo. On his own.

And that just might demolish both of them.

It was eight thirty and Behr was ready for bed. He wasn't sure if that was a sign of age, his brain injury, or the fact that he'd camped out with twenty-five teen boys last night who had swapped stories around the fire long after the sun had set. They'd been as chatty as his sisters when they got together.

Behr filled a glass with water and Margo followed him into the bedroom. She sat by the side of the bed, watching him. He'd let her out to potty a few minutes ago.

"You're just going to sit there and watch me, huh?"

Margo's head tilted as if she was trying to understand.

"I'm thinking about having you sleep in the living room. I'm nervous I'm going to wake up in the middle of the night and find you staring at me."

Margo dropped to the floor, resting her chin on her paws. Behr didn't have a dog bed yet, so he'd grabbed an old blanket for her to lie on.

"But I suppose having you out there with the door shut defeats the purpose of having you at all. The whole reason is for you to help me if needed, right?"

Margo blinked. Glanced away. Checked back. She was probably just as tired as he was. It had been a long night for their first experience together.

Behr settled against the headboard, pillows propped behind him. He could watch a little TV. That usually helped him drift off. But it wasn't getting to sleep that was hard for him. It was the middle-of-the-night panic and nightmares that woke him.

His heart revved and then hiccupped in his chest, the rhythm sloppy, anxious. Being alone with Margo was a huge trigger. And yet she was as calm as ever. Which only made him feel as weak as cheap, canned spaghetti sauce. Who was scared of the sweetest brown Lab on planet earth?

As long as Behr could see Margo and knew where she was, what she was doing, he was fine. He'd grown accustomed to her in that way. But now he was supposed to sleep with her in his place? He was upset at Ellery for putting him in this position.

No—he was mad at himself for not being able to handle it.

And the only person he wanted to talk to about it was Ellery.

He snagged his phone off the nightstand and rattled off a text.

How's Fletcher doing? I can't believe how exhausted I am.

Ellery answered quickly. He fell asleep on the couch about ten minutes ago. I think I'm just going to leave him there for the night. Not like I can move him. **Another text quickly followed.** How's it going over there?

Going fine. I'm a wuss. When did I turn into this version of myself? I used to be so capable.

You're still capable. You're just climbing the mountain right now. When you get to the top, it will be worth it.

This mountain seems to be growing.

There was a pause before she answered again. Do you need me to come over and hang out for a bit?

Did he want Ellery here? Yes. Because of Margo? Not exactly. He wanted her for himself. Wanted to engage in another hug like the one this morning. Wanted to see her eyes grow confused and light up when he teased her. Wanted to hold her hand and know that everything was going to be okay.

Thanks for offering, but we're doing all right. I'm just a little nervous. Keyed up. The fact that he could admit his inadequacies to Ellery wasn't lost on him. She'd burrowed into his world like Margo when she curled into herself to sleep, and Behr had no interest in extricating her.

Just as he sent the text, Margo's head appeared next to him. She laid her chin on his arm like a warm, weighted blanket.

Careful not to dislodge her, he texted again. And now she's comforting me. I didn't say any of that out loud. How does she know?

It's her job to know.

Behr wanted to continue texting—to ask Ellery about her day, what she'd done last night—but his weariness was winning. And she probably had more interesting things to do than text with him on a Saturday night.

He was doing better now that he'd communicated with Ellery. She calmed him. And made him happy, according to Dad. The man wasn't wrong about that.

Normally at this point, when Behr was days

away from seeing Marina and the kids, he'd be occupied with thoughts of them. They would be all-consuming to him. His only focus. Instead, he didn't want to leave the state of Colorado. And there was only one reason he could think of for that—and it started with an E and ended with a why-did-she-have-this-effect-on-him. And how was he going to get his head back in the game? The game that supported Jake's family when Jake wasn't able to do that himself.

The game that Behr used to be winning and now was forgetting to play.

Chapter Fifteen

Enduring the long weekend while Behr was gone to visit Marina and the kids without hearing from him had morphed Ellery into a bundle of apprehension and impatience.

That camping night after MENtor camp paled in comparison to this.

Brynn sidled up to her in the kitchen. "Your nerves are making me nervous."

"Am I that obvious?" Ellery winced. She'd hoped that she was doing a better job of hiding the bees buzzing frantically in her stomach every time she heard a noise out front and got her hopes up that it was Behr arriving for Fletcher's party.

The teen's upcoming birthday in two weeks was the technical reason for the Monday night celebration, but for Ellery and Desiree and probably every other adult attending, the evening was also a nod to Fletcher completing MENtor camp. He'd come out of the program more able to see the world around him and had retired a good portion of his anger, though he could still play the sullen teenager card like a professional when he believed the occasion called for it. But leaning toward acting like a typical teenager instead of the heading-for-juvie kind was a plus. A huge one.

"Have you talked to him at all this weekend?" Brynn stole the ice tray from Ellery's hand and took over the job of dumping it into the bin in the freezer. Probably because Ellery had just been staring at the tray like it was an advanced algebra equation.

"No." There was no point in pretending she didn't know Brynn was referring to Behr. She moved to stir the vegetable dip that had already been fully mixed. "He was only gone Thursday to Sunday. And then he worked today. Of course I didn't bug him."

Ellery had wanted to give Behr space. She'd wanted to pretend she wasn't intensely, debilitatingly curious over how his trip was going—with Margo *and* Marina.

After his hesitance to take Margo home last Saturday, Ellery had never expected him to rebound the way he had. On Monday, he'd had a lunchtime session with Kapp, and he'd come out of it with a new sense of determination. He'd asked Ellery to help him with the logistics of taking Margo on the trip to Louisiana.

She'd been floored, excited and every emotion in between.

After work on Monday, Tuesday and Wednesday they'd crammed in longer sessions in order to give Behr confidence in his handling skills.

Despite any remaining fears of his, he'd been fully committed. She was incredibly proud of him. He was one strong soldier despite the fact that he considered himself the weakest link.

And then came Marina… Ellery had seen the woman's picture. She was stunning, with beautiful brown skin, toffee eyes, fantastic tight coils. Even in pictures she had a light about her—an essence. Add in their intense emotional connection, and it was a wonder they *weren't* together. Behr had reiterated there was nothing romantic between them, but what if something changed on this trip?

"I sound like his sisters." Though she felt anything but sisterly toward Behr. Ellery might not be at a point in her life that she could entertain a romantic relationship with Behr, but to watch something like that develop between him and Marina would be a horse-sized pill to swallow.

"What?"

"Nothing." Ellery picked up the stack of napkins and instantly dropped them. She knelt to gather the mess.

Brynn moved on to the next tray and added it to the bin. "You're as bad as a teenager obsessed with a crush."

"I am not obsessed." Ellery adjusted the napkins so the edges were flush and returned them to the counter. She would just like to confirm that Behr and Margo had survived their first trip. That was all. Or at least most of it. "Plus, Fletcher is a teenager, and he doesn't have a crush. He's not obsessed with anyone."

Ellery nudged Brynn out of her way so she could retrieve the homemade potato salad from the fridge. She'd had a lot of time on her hands over the weekend. And she'd spent much of it on an emotional roller coaster, because on Friday night, Nico had attempted suicide. The move had left his family frightened and Ellery more determined than ever to not let another veteran navigate the trauma alone the way Nico currently was. Having a possible second local business interested in being a consistent donor was a huge leap in getting to that place.

"I feel like your statement about teenagers is generalized and offensive to the group as a whole." Ellery engaged in her best hoity-toity tone, and Brynn laughed. "Including the one currently on the back deck dutifully filling his mother in on the last week of his life."

"The boy who was such a mess that his mom shipped him off to you like a last-second, long shot pass? The one who, after his arrival, made me fear you were going to start tearing out your perfectly colored hair? That boy?"

"That's the one."

"Well done, Fletch." Brynn returned the last tray filled with water to the freezer and then stilled in place, her ear perked, head slanted like one of the dogs would do. "I think I just heard a car." She peeked out the front window. "It's Behr."

"I'm going to set out the food so everyone can eat buffet style when they get here."

"You heard me, correct?"

Ellery nodded. It would be weird to burst out the front door right when Behr arrived…*like I did after the camping trip.* Exactly. Ellery had one tiny smidgeon of chill left in her, and she planned to milk that drop for all it was worth. She could wait for Behr to enter the house.

Brynn grasped Ellery's shoulders and turned her toward the front door. "Go. I'll handle the food. Make sure he's okay so you can think about something else besides him and Nico this evening."

Brynn had been amazing this weekend with

the Nico news. Supportive. Encouraging. She and Ellery had consumed a tub of ice cream on Saturday night in the name of emotional eating. It had eased the sting a bit.

Her friend gave her a gentle shove as additional incentive.

"All right. All right! I'm going." There was no fighting Brynn. Or the current that moved Ellery with invisible force toward the man who'd inhabited her mind all weekend.

Behr was letting Margo out of the car when Ellery stepped outside. He'd trimmed his hair since she last saw him, and when he turned, he looked younger, more confident...more something.

Her heart rammed against her ribs.

She approached, the sun-warmed asphalt welcome against her bare feet. "How was the trip? Did everything go okay?"

"Hi." His grin hitched up, up, until Ellery was lost in it. "Usually people greet each other instead of launching into an instant inquisition."

"Hi, Behr." She ran a hand over Margo's mug. "Hi, Margo-girl. There. Is that better?"

"Better." Behr studied her rather intensely. What was that about? "It's also common for people to hug after one of them returns from a trip. Or so I've read in my etiquette books." His continued attention sent a wave of warmth down to her toes that began ricocheting from one limb to another like a bouncy ball.

"Your collection of those is impressive."

"It really is." His gaze held all kinds of softness she wanted to dissect. "I missed you, Ellery."

The comment was so serious and blatant, so outside of their normal banter, that Ellery's jaw loosened. Behr had erected a safety net between their hearts since the start, just like she had. What had happened to change that?

"Did you miss my bossiness most? Or my help with Margo? Or my bright, joyful countenance?" She'd turned into Behr, teasing about everything, refusing to enter the serious zone he'd just crashed into.

"All of the above." He stepped closer and opened his arms, and Ellery's body oozed in his direction like a child's toy slime meeting gravity. And then they were embracing. Turned out discussing said embrace beforehand did not detract from the merit of it. She inhaled his scent—clean and crisp and Behr—and never wanted to move again. She could eat, sleep and work from this position, right?

Maybe she had actually morphed into a teenager. Ellery couldn't remember the last time, if ever, that she'd missed someone in a matter of days. Or that she'd craved being with someone as intensely as she did Behr.

Felt like that could be a huge problem based on their "friends only" relationship status.

He let go, and Ellery forced herself to retreat. "So, how was the weekend?"

Did something happen between you and Marina? Rip it off like a Band-Aid so I can get to the handling-it part.

Behr glanced to the street as his parents' vehicle rolled into the driveway and then Alessandra's followed with her crew.

"I want to hear about your weekend, too, but we'll have to talk later, I guess."

"Sure. That's great." *Lies!* Ellery was dying to know what had happened. She wanted to borrow Fletcher's teenager card and throw a fit—or throw out all the people currently pouring out of vehicles so that she could hear what Behr had to say.

But since she was *technically* an adult, she would resist doing any of those things.

At least for the time being.

"I can't thank you enough, Behr. You changed my son's life. You saved him. And me." Desiree had cornered Behr fifteen minutes prior and had been gushing ever since.

"*I* didn't do anything. It was MENtor camp.

And God." Really, that was where the credit needed to go.

"He wouldn't have had the opportunity without you." Desiree swiped a tear. "I'm sorry for getting emotional. It's just, I've been praying for that boy since before he was born, and these last few weeks have finally, *finally* felt like answers. I guess I needed that more than I realized. My faith needed the reminder that God hears my prayers."

"I understand that. I'm so glad he's been affected the way he has." Behr hadn't expected a career at Step Up, but now he couldn't imagine not having it. The place and the kids gave him purpose. Made it worth getting out of bed after a rough night or an incapacitating headache.

Ellery had been flitting around the party all evening, checking on people, refilling drinks, making sure there was enough food. She popped over to him and Desiree now.

"Des, can I borrow him for a sec?" she asked apologetically. Her fingers grazed Behr's arm and he turned to liquid. How could such a simple touch level him so quickly?

"Of course." Desiree moved over to the group sitting on the living room couches, and Ellery pulled Behr to the corner of the room.

If she wanted to make out, he was game.

Though his thought would likely completely shock her.

He'd tried holding himself in check when he'd first arrived tonight while also hinting that things had changed—at least for him. He'd probably only confused her.

"What's up?"

"I'm going to bring in Fletcher's surprise." She kept her volume low, but her excitement was palpable. "Hank is out back. Fletcher's been asking about his dog ever since finishing the program, but Desiree and I thought it would be fun to combine it with his birthday and give him the dog tonight. She picked up a bunch of supplies already for him." Ellery's beauty only increased when she was happy. And the happiness was currently infiltrating every part of her. She was so good, right down to the very last drop. What an amazing human being to be this thrilled to surprise her snarky teenage nephew. Not that Fletcher hadn't shown major improvement.

"You need my help?"

"No." Her expression flashed with humor and warmth and caring. "I wanted to warn you I'm going to bring him in. I didn't want to mess you up by surprising you with yet another dog."

Of course. It was so Ellery to have a packed house and be thinking about his dog issues.

She'd kept Dash in the basement for the party, but that was because Dash didn't do people or crowds well. Behr appreciated that Dash stayed in his corner of the ring and allowed Behr to stay in his.

They were wary allies, the two of them.

"I wondered if you'd want to wait out on the deck while I bring him in."

"I can do that. And then if he's calm, I can probably come back in as long as I have Margo."

More of that bright, cheery sunshine spilled from Ellery. "Perfect! I'll be back in a few."

Behr moved onto the deck with Margo. Alessandra and Brynn were out there, but they were in an intense conversation with another couple, so Behr stole a second to himself by the railing.

He got there in time to see Ellery streaming down to the kennels, anticipation evident in every step. She'd added wellies to her sundress for the trek across the yard, and the combination only made her more adorable.

Behr hadn't intended to reveal everything he was feeling the minute he'd arrived tonight, but seeing Ellery scoot down the front steps in that flowered dress, barefoot, beautiful, happy to see him…he'd had to hold her, even if it was only for a few seconds.

He'd likely given himself away, but Ellery hadn't objected. He was almost certain she'd inhaled him while he'd been resisting pressing a kiss to the crown of her head.

Everything had changed in Louisiana. Everything. And Behr wanted to tell Ellery about it.

They'd had an agreement from the start to forge a friendship and only that, but Behr was interested in making major adjustments to that verbal contract. What he didn't know was how Ellery would react.

Would tipping the scales of their relationship toward romantic work? Or would it upset the whole system?

He didn't want to lose her, but it would be herculean tough to resist pursuing more with her after learning what he had while on his trip.

Marina was engaged. She was moving on, moving forward. And she wanted Behr to do the same. Ever since Marina had bombarded Behr with the news, he'd gone through the gamut of emotions. Shock. Concern. Cautious hope. He'd spent time with Marina and Kurt over the weekend and witnessed firsthand how much they loved each other. How they worked in tandem. The kids loved Kurt. Marina loved Kurt. Behr had been left with no choice but to embrace the man who would take Jake's place. Marina had assured him she still loved Jake. Always would. But she'd been determined to move forward for her own sake and for the kids. And for Behr's sake, too. She'd witnessed how he'd gone stagnant because he was so focused on them. She'd wanted to prove to both of them that there was more than just survival after grief. And she'd done it. Behr had savored every minute with the kids because he'd known his role with them would never be the same. He'd be a distant uncle from now on. Someone who'd been friends with the kids' birth father. And he should rejoice in that. He was. He did. He was glad for them. It would take him some time to adjust his role in their lives, but he would do it for their sakes. He refused to be the one to put a damper on their new contentment.

Marina had talked to Behr before he'd left for the airport and begged him to start living again. To be free of any burden regarding Jake's passing. She'd glowed with peace. Behr had assured her he would do his best.

And then on the plane, he'd known exactly what that meant for him. Ellery. He'd been holding back with her because of his commitment to Marina and the kids. But now that things had shifted, changed, he was free to entertain feelings for her. Feelings that had been there the whole time, but that he'd shoved down, buried, tried to ignore.

Ellery reemerged from the training building with Hank—the rambunctious German shorthaired pointer mix for Fletcher. That shouldn't amuse Behr so much, but it did. Fletch would have his hands full. But being occupied by Hank would definitely be a good thing and should help keep him out of trouble.

The dog reveal was a hit—Fletcher was obviously floored and thrilled by Hank, though he would never use either of those words. The party was a success, and under the guise of helping clean up, Behr stayed until everyone else left, when really, he just wanted more time with Ellery.

Brynn had planned to stay to assist, too, but when she'd taken notice of the fact that it was just her, Behr and Ellery still present, she'd skedaddled out of there, making Behr equal parts curious just how obvious his feelings for Ellery were and tempted to write Brynn a thank-you note for her hasty exit.

"Behr, you really don't have to help me clean up." Ellery spoke from her perch at the sink, which was filled with soaking dishes. "Most of it is done."

Most. Some was a better description.

He tossed a used stack of disposable cups into the trash can. "This way it will all be done and you won't have to do it yourself. We both know Fletcher isn't going to be volunteering to help."

Though the teen had taken Hank and Dash outside to play with them.

"Ha! That is true." She rinsed a platter and loaded it in the dishwasher. "Well, if you're staying, the least you could do is tell me about your trip."

Behr grabbed the dishcloth and wiped the counters. Margo, trying to be helpful, trailed him. She was liable to trip him if she kept it up. Behr directed her to lie by the kitchen entrance and then returned to cleaning.

Ellery beamed as she nodded toward the dog. "You look like an old pro with her."

"I'm not sure *pro* is the right word." Behr was slowly adjusting to having a service dog, and Margo was adjusting to him, too. After his first night, after he'd panicked, things had gone smoothly. He'd slept all through that night—the first in a long time. He'd decided the next morning that Ellery was right—Margo was his perfect match. After that, he'd been even more determined to adjust to her. To maximize her potential for him. He'd talked to Kapp. He'd planned to include Margo in his travel and had orchestrated that along with Ellery's assistance. He'd done it. Was doing it.

"I wouldn't have her at all if you hadn't forced me into trying."

Ellery waved a hand, likely about to disregard the compliment, but Behr scooted forward fast enough to catch it and stop the movement.

Their linked hands swung down between them and then separated.

Ellery's gaze had widened at his touch. At how close they were. Her mouth formed that little O she was so fond of, and her eyes pooled with questions. When they skimmed down to his mouth and bounced away, it took everything in Behr not to lean forward and make good on that fleeting glance.

"What in the world happened on that trip?"

Funny that she knew him so well. He was acting different. He'd been given a free pass to do so, and…it felt like right where he was supposed to be all along.

Behr should probably create some space between them, but he didn't.

"Marina is engaged."

"She is? And you didn't know?"

His head shook. "She told me she had news to share with me when I got there. She'd mentioned she was dating someone a few months back, but I didn't realize how serious it was. She said it happened fast. A little over five months they've been together. She wanted me to meet him. He's great. He's not Jake, but that's on me and my issues. The kids, Marina, everyone is happy."

"That is *huge* news."

"Isn't it?"

"I have to admit, I kept thinking that you'd come back, and you and Marina would be…"

"That we would be what?"

"Together." Ellery focused on the sink full of dishes and began scrubbing a pan that had held brownies. "That you'd both somehow decide enough time had passed and you were interested in each other."

"How could that happen when the person I'm most interested in is standing right in front of me? Marina told me to go live, and the first thing—the only thing—that came to mind was you." There. He'd leveled with her.

She faced him, her hands dripping with dishwater. "What?"

Behr edged closer, his palms sneaking up to cradle her cheeks. "Ellery." He didn't know what else to say. She had to see how he felt, didn't she?

Her sudsy fingers wrapped around his wrists, and she went up on her tiptoes to meet his kiss. Her arms wrapped around his neck like they'd been waiting to fill that spot, and Behr was gone. He couldn't believe he'd held out on recognizing or admitting how he'd felt about Ellery pretty much from the moment he'd met her.

Margo let out a whine, almost as if she was

embarrassed to be witnessing such a display. They laughed, but Behr didn't move far. Now that he'd kicked open the door to kissing Ellery, he never wanted to close it. She tasted like dessert and peaches and home all rolled into one strangely irresistible dish.

He was reconfirming those details with another kiss when the front door opened, the dogs made a ruckus, and Fletcher appeared at the entrance to the kitchen.

"No girls while you're in the program!" the teen quipped, both dogs thankfully on leashes and under his control.

Behr wasn't sure at exactly what point during the last few developments Ellery had leaped across the kitchen like a gazelle, but she had to have put five feet between them in an instant.

"Speaking of girls," Fletcher continued, "I've been texting with Raven since the program finished. We're going to the rodeo in town on Friday night, since that is all Mt. Vista has to offer in terms of entertainment." Fletcher continued down the stairs with both dogs as if he hadn't just interrupted their kiss, dropped a bomb on them and left Ellery mortified, her face rocking first-day-at-the-beach sunburn levels.

"The girl from the horse stables? I guess he does have a teenage crush." Ellery's hands covered her cheeks. "I can't believe that just happened."

"Which part?"

"All of it!"

A chuckle escaped.

Ellery whacked him in the biceps. Had about as much impact as a fly landing. "Behr! That was embarrassing! Why aren't you embarrassed?"

"I'm more focused on doing it again."

"Behr!" His name came out as a screech.

"I probably should have done a better job of explaining myself first, but you were right there, and I couldn't resist you."

Her hands lowered to her hips, her mouth curving. "Huh. I kinda like the sound of that."

"Everything changed when Marina told me her news. It was like she set me free in a way. I mean, you know we weren't romantically involved, but I was committed to them."

"And I understood it." Another reason she was amazing. "So, what are you saying, exactly?"

"When Marina told me about Kurt, you were my first thought. I'm tired of pretending that I wasn't attracted to you from the start. That I wasn't tempted to do what we just did all along." Phew. That had all just spilled right out.

Ellery's head shook. Why was it shaking? "I wanted to hear you say that, and yet—"

And yet. Behr's system crashed like he'd been without food or water for weeks.

"I can't, Behr."

"I'm pretty sure we can and just did."

Her short laugh was quiet and sad and nothing like her usual sugary confetti.

"Your commitments have changed, but mine haven't. I didn't tell you this while you were gone, but Nico attempted suicide on Friday night."

Oh, man. That was terrible. "Ellery, I'm so sorry." He reached out, squeezed her hand.

"I hadn't found him a dog yet. Still don't have one for him."

"*Ellery.* His attempted suicide is not on you. You know that, right?"

"I know that in theory." She tapped a fist against her sternum. "But not in here. I don't know how to stop giving my all to this place. To saving them." Her speech dipped and rose with emotion. "The way I wish someone could have for Ace. And Jake."

Jake's name was like a machete tearing through his gut. Behr understood it. Her. All of it. How could he not?

"I don't want you to stop saving anyone. But you don't have to do it alone. It's okay to have a partner in life, Ellery. I'm not asking you to choose between me and Helping Paws. I'm asking you to let me help you. Support you."

Tears brimmed in those spring green eyes. Behr couldn't handle that. He tugged her close, and Ellery collapsed against his chest like she'd just run a marathon.

"I'm not saying I don't have feelings for you." Her response was muffled against his shirt. "Obviously I do."

He pressed his teeth together to keep from arguing with her, convincing her. She had to want him back of her own accord, her own choice. He just held her tighter, hoping the physical would translate.

"I just... I can't right now. I've got a second line of funding possibly coming our way and proving our worth to them is taking all my time and energy. Plus, Fletcher is only staying this week, and I need to concentrate on him. Nothing has changed."

"Everything has changed." The statement came out more bitter than Behr had intended. He'd had time to process after seeing Marina. Shouldn't he allow Ellery the same?

She eased back slightly, her hands sliding down his arms, holding on. "I'm sorry that I can't leap into a relationship right now, but Behr, I can't lose you. Please don't disappear."

"You're not going to lose me." Even as he said it, the words jumped back to bite him. Now that he'd let himself go *there* with Ellery, how could he backtrack? "I just might need some time and space to re-friend-zone myself." To figure out how to stop the train he was on that was traveling at lightning speeds toward far more than like. He was at the station for love, and Behr had wanted, for the first time ever, to get off, stay a while or a lifetime. Experience every day with someone who supported him like Ellery did. Who saw him and loved him back. But she wasn't even at the same tracks as he was.

Did he support her as well as she did him? He was going to have to look into that, because if he did, she wouldn't even be entertaining the questions she was.

"How can I even ask you for that?"

She could ask him for anything, it seemed, because even this, he would do his best to give her. "We'll figure it out. Promise. Just give me a little room to do that." They would navigate this together—somehow—right after they took some time apart.

Chapter Sixteen

Ellery's hand shook as she waited for the phone to be answered or go to voice mail. Option number two happened, and she listened for the tone before lurching into her speech.

"Mr. Bengal, I received your message, and I am so sorry for missing our meeting. I had entered it into my calendar as an hour after what we'd discussed by accident, and I cannot apologize enough. I'd still very much like to partner with your company, and I hope we can reschedule." Ellery hung up before she could blubber on about her mistake or the lives it could affect. What was happening to her?

In the five days since Behr had changed everything in their relationship by admitting he had feelings for her—and kissing her like she was precious, needed, wanted—Ellery had botched up this morning's very important meeting, rushed into finding a dog for Nico that had turned out to be all wrong, and snapped at a volunteer, which she never, ever did.

She was unraveling, big-time.

Leaning back in her chair, she raised arms over her head and let out a yelp of frustration.

Fletcher's bedroom door opened. He came down the hallway cautiously, like he didn't know what he'd find. A mountain lion. Intruder. Den of snakes.

"You okay?"

"Kinda not."

"Kinda figured."

"Sorry about the war cry. Before you lived here, I tended to release frustration by just… letting it out. Weird, right? But it just helps for some reason. And while you were living here, I managed to corral it, but today has just been one of those days."

Fletcher glanced upstairs. "Didn't we just finish eating breakfast fifteen minutes ago?"

Ellery had made his favorite—chocolate chip pancakes. He'd even stayed at the table with her until she was finished eating. A sort of parting gift to her, she imagined. She'd had the Bengal Construction phone call scheduled for a Saturday morning because that was when Trip Bengal could squeeze it in, and then she and Fletcher had planned to head for Denver, Desiree and home.

"I missed an important meeting." When Ellery had headed downstairs to go over her notes and call Mr. Bengal, she'd realized that she had two missed calls from him. Her phone had been on silent, and she'd been making breakfast, hanging with Fletcher on his last morning with her. Mr. Bengal's voicemail had revealed that she'd written the time down wrong in her calendar somehow. Ellery was mortified and devastated. And then of course Mr. Bengal hadn't answered when she'd tried him back. But why would he? She'd had the time wrong, and he'd moved on in his schedule.

Fletcher winced. "I'm sorry about your thing."

"It's not a big deal." Felt as crushing as the earth resting on her chest, but she'd put it aside for now. "How's packing?"

"Good. Almost done."

"Knock, knock," Brynn called from upstairs, and her footsteps quickly followed. "I let myself in since the door was unlocked." She handed a blended mocha to Fletcher. "Trade. One sugary drink for the car ride in exchange for one goodbye hug."

His mouth lifted, and he hugged her willingly.

"Gonna miss you, Fletch. You sure made things interesting around here."

His shoulders lifted. "That's kind of my job as a teenager."

She laughed.

"Fletcher's just finishing packing and then we're going to take off."

Brynn hugged him again, this time without permission, not that Fletcher seemed to mind. "I'll see you again. Soon."

"I'll definitely be back to visit."

"Fletcher's desire to return to Mt. Vista has nothing to do with me or you, Brynn, and everything to do with his new crush. Raven." Ellery stretched out the name like a third grader would.

His face turned neon pink. "Gotta finish packing! Thanks for the drink, Brynn." He bounded down the hallway, intent on escape.

"Anytime." She held out the iced coffee in her other hand to Ellery.

"For me?"

"Did you really think I'd bring something for Fletch and not you?"

Sweet Brynn. Ellery accepted the drink. "Thank you." She infused cheer into her gratitude, but it fell as flat as a pancake without baking powder.

"You sound like you lost your best friend, but I'm right here, so that can't be the issue." Brynn dropped into the chair across from Ellery's desk. The one Behr had occupied when he'd come for his first training session. "What's going on? Are you stressing about dropping off Fletcher?"

"Yes and no. It's the right timing for taking him home." He would start a new school year in about a month, and he was ready to make his own way thanks to MENtor camp…and thanks to Behr and Case and Rome and God and a whole list of others who'd prayed for him. Ellery knew he was going to be all right, though there would be bumps in the road. She couldn't believe she was going to miss the kid who'd tormented her when he'd first arrived. Who would grunt answers at her now?

"I dropped the ball on the Bengal Construction meeting. I put it in my calendar wrong." She sipped the cool, creamy concoction from the straw, but it tasted like dirt and water mixed in a toy blender.

"I'm sure they'll let you reschedule. It happens to everyone once in a while."

"What if they think I'm inept? That not being able to manage a schedule also means I won't manage their donations wisely?"

"That's a pretty big stretch."

Was it? Panic and adrenaline raced through Ellery's veins. Ever since Behr had left last Monday night, she'd had trouble sleeping. Thinking. Not hurting in the depths of her spirit. She missed him an outlandish amount. He'd asked her to give him time to re-friend-zone himself, as he'd called it, and she was. But it was hard. Not seeing him was difficult. She'd grown so attached to him. She wanted more kisses. More of all he'd offered. But today was proof that she couldn't get distracted. How much worse would she have botched things up this week if they were romantically involved? She couldn't lose focus on Helping Paws in that way. The charity couldn't suffer because her heart was sorely tempted to grab hold of Behr and never let go.

"What else is going on?" Brynn questioned.

"I'm overwhelmed. We got so many applicants over the last few weeks that I'm considering closing the waiting list completely until we get caught up. There's such a need, and I'm—"

"One person with a handful of volunteers. You need some help around here, Elle. You can't keep doing all of this on your own."

Ellery resisted another panicked wail. "That's what the funding was for. I thought maybe we could hire someone for the office with it. And use a portion to recruit more volunteer trainers, which would mean more dogs, more matches." The compassionate souls who trained service dogs for veterans in their homes were the bread and butter that made Helping Paws possible.

"Didn't you already get one company to donate for the year?"

"Yes, but two is better than one."

Brynn's laugh was dry. "Now, that is true."

Ellery inhaled another sip. The coffee tasted sweet this time. Less like mud. "What is going on with me? I'm never like this."

"It could be…" Brynn's fingers steepled against the desk. "Now hear me out. It *could be* because you turned down the guy you've fallen for in order to keep juggling all of the balls in your world by yourself. I seem to recall he offered to help with those."

"That can't be it." Ellery's attempt at a smile quickly morphed into a frown. "I thought I was doing the right thing. I thought if I could just concentrate on Helping Paws long enough, it would be successful and help more people."

"It is accomplishing both of those things and will continue to. The real question is how long you're going to be able to keep going like this, without support, without a life outside of this place. Without an office that's separate from your house that you can go to, then leave and check out when you go home. What you're attempting here is amazing, Elle. But you're going to burn out if you keep going like this."

She already felt the singeing, the heat. And Ellery really didn't want to go down like that.

"How many times have I brought this up to you?"

Ellery played with the straw in her drink, her reply quiet and accompanied by a sigh. "More than I can count."

Brynn raised her palms in a see-what-I'm-saying gesture. "Exactly."

Behr had sought refuge at his parents' house, which, based on the noise level inside, didn't seem logical. But there was something comforting about the chaos.

His sister Jana and her three kids had driven down from Fort Collins for the day, and Mom had planned a big dinner. Behr had helped in the kitchen for a while, but Alessandra had just kicked him out for not cutting the vegetables thin enough. And that was after pestering him about Ellery. *What happened? Why weren't we allowed to invite her tonight? Whatever you did, Behr, you should fix it. We love Ellery.* He did, too. That was part of the problem.

He stepped onto the back porch to find Dad in his favorite chair. Smart man.

"How do you always manage to escape before they get their clutches in you?"

"Many years of practice." Dad motioned for Behr to take the chair next to him. "I'm on deck for cleanup duty. It's quieter and I'll have the kitchen to myself."

Again, smart man.

Behr took a seat and Margo settled next to him, her eyelids quickly drooping. He hadn't slept well last night, which meant she hadn't, either. Margo was always on, always in tune with him.

"Are Ellery and Fletcher coming tonight?" Dad asked. "I thought Mom mentioned inviting them."

Thankfully, she'd mentioned the same to Behr and he'd been able to put the kibosh on that offer before Mom made things weird for both of them.

"No. I think Ellery is driving Fletcher back to his mom's today." Behr had gleaned that information from his nephews, who'd seen Fletcher numerous times this past week. He didn't like not knowing what Ellery and Fletcher were up to—how they were doing.

How was Ellery handling Fletcher's departure? Was she relieved? Sad? Some of each? Would she need someone to process with after dropping him off? A week ago that might have been Behr, but today she'd reach out to Brynn, no doubt.

Behr's request for space had likely hurt Ellery, but he wasn't sure how else to handle the situation. She both wanted him in her life and didn't want him. Painful combination.

"Everything okay?" Dad's intense gaze was on Behr. How long had he been studying him?

Behr had never talked to his dad about a woman before—not that there'd been that many of them—but Dad's insight into his friendship with Ellery last time made Behr more willing to open up.

"Ellery and I weren't even dating but we broke up." Didn't that about sum it up?

"I don't understand."

"She's not interested in dating anyone. She has too much going on with work." *Or this broken version of me is more of a hindrance than a help.* Behr hadn't even realized he was harboring a thought like that until it spilled right out onto his parents' back porch. It was hard not to believe that Ellery's disinterest in him— even though she'd claimed to be interested— was because of his *stuff.* His issues. He wasn't whole. Hadn't been since his accident and probably never would be. He had headaches that took him down for the count. His vision blurred when he overtaxed himself. He was sensitive to light and noise, and overdoing it at a far greater level than he had been before his injury. His balance was greatly helped by Margo, but that didn't change his body or its capabilities.

"I understand her work requiring a lot from her," Behr continued. "She has such a heart for veterans. How can I fault her for that?"

"Don't fault her. Help her."

"I tried."

"How?"

By telling her that he would support her… and then disappearing when she said she wasn't ready to take their relationship to another level.

"What do I do? How do I show her I'll help and not hinder her work? Do I go out and get donations? Dog trainers? What?"

"Have you prayed for her?"

Behr swallowed. "Yes." But mostly he'd prayed that she would change her mind. Selfish.

He was starting to see Dad's point.

"What else?" he asked quietly so that none of the women in the house overheard. Between Mom and Alessandra, Behr was advised out at this point. Dad had a pass because he was pretty much wisdom personified.

"Instead of trying to help her in order to gain something for yourself, just love her, no strings attached. Be there for her. God will work out the rest. Either He'll change your heart, or hers."

Could it really be that simple? The concept gave Behr peace because it would allow him to support Ellery and stop focusing on himself.

And if it made him half the man his father was, Behr would call it a win.

No matter the outcome.

At first Ellery had assumed the incidents were just coincidences.

A new volunteer—a retired military wife and a friend of Behr's mom—asking if she could volunteer in the office at Helping Paws fifteen hours a week.

Behr's parents letting her know they were prayerfully considering applying to train service dogs for the charity.

Brynn taking Ellery for a pedicure and paying for hers because a Good Samaritan had given her a gift certificate for it.

But when Ellery had walked up to the church for Nico's funeral, who'd passed away unexpectedly but peacefully in his sleep from cardiac arrhythmia the day after she'd returned Fletcher to Denver, to find Behr and Margo standing outside the doors waiting for her…waiting to be her no-expectations emotional support system…she'd known.

Behr was quietly and unassumingly behind all of it.

He might not be eating dinner with her in the evening or texting her throughout the day, but he was keeping his promise not to walk out of her life.

After the funeral yesterday afternoon, Ellery had wondered if Behr would say something to her. Ask if her feelings had changed or try to kiss her again.

He'd done none of the above, though he had held her for a long spell after the service while she'd cried for Nico and Ace and Jake and all the rest—plus the ones they'd left behind.

Ellery had woken this morning and known in the depths of her soul that the war she'd been waging on her own had to end. She needed someone in this battle with her, and she wanted Behr. Missed Behr. Needed Behr.

He'd certainly proved that he wasn't the leaving kind.

It was time to let go, to trust, to find her way back to *living* after Ace—not just devoting every ounce of her energy to honoring him.

And her theory about Helping Paws suffering if she was focused on a relationship with Behr was obviously way off, as Brynn had been pointing out to her on the daily. Because she'd done plenty of messing up in his absence, though thankfully the rescheduled meeting with Trip Bengal had gone well. He'd committed his business to supporting the charity for not just one, but two years. A huge relief that gave Ellery the confidence to hire and allowed her to improve Helping Paws in numerous ways.

The idea that she could be a better, more capable, more successful, happier version of herself with Behr, with his support, his love, was absolutely freeing.

She'd waited impatiently until Behr would be off work today to go talk to him, but he hadn't been at his place. Knocking down his door hadn't worked this time. Ellery had even gone so far as to consider driving by his parents' house, but it was too secluded for her not to get caught. Besides, if he was there, what was she going to do? Bang on their front door?

Even in her state of desperation to see him, she wouldn't do that.

She drove to the overlook instead of home, needing the solace of it. The space to pray. But when she reached the turnoff, Behr's vehicle was parked there.

"Well played, God."

She exited her truck and found Behr exactly where he'd been when she'd brought him here, only this time, his legs were hanging over the cliff. Because she hadn't been here to mother him.

"Don't fall. I'd hate to have to tell your family my favorite spot was your demise."

He twisted in her direction, that playful, teasing grin igniting. "Hey." He radiated peace. Ellery wanted to steal a scoop for herself. In fact, she planned to if Behr was still game. Because she was so *done* doing life on her own.

He patted the ground next to him, on the side not occupied by Margo, and Ellery copped a seat, sending her legs over the edge, too. Living included sitting on the edge of a cliff, apparently.

"I'm in your spot." His countenance switched to chagrined. "I didn't know you'd be here. Sorry. I was about to go anyway."

"You don't need to scramble out of here."

Those caramel eyes held hers. "I don't?"

"No. I actually just came from looking for you."

Now those eyes widened. "You did?"

"I went all Incredible Hulk on your front door, and you weren't even there to enjoy it."

His low chuckle melted her like one of those videos of a military dad coming home, surprising their kid.

"I'm disappointed I missed that. Is everything okay? Any particular reason why you were looking for me?"

Her heart reverberated in her chest as fast as Fletcher's dog Hank could sprint across a football field.

"Yes, as a matter of fact, there is. Was." Ellery had mapped out what she wanted to say, but now that she'd finally stumbled upon Behr, she couldn't recall any of it.

"And…" Behr leaned in her direction. Ellery's body was a magnet for his, shifting his way. He'd kissed her in lieu of explaining everything after he'd been to visit Marina and the kids. Would it be so wrong for her to follow suit?

She knew the instant his grin erupted because she'd been memorizing his mouth. That grin also said he'd noticed said memorizing. His finger tucked under her chin, propping her gaze to his. "You figured out you can't live without me, either, didn't ya, kid?"

She nodded.

"It's *about time*." His lips captured her laughter, and Ellery sank into him, her fingers grazing the stubble on his cheeks, sliding behind his neck, wrapping her whole self into him, because that was where she wanted to be. Had always wanted to be. How had she waited so long to admit the truth? To accept it? How had she functioned without the one person who loved her so well that he'd loved her—action-verb style—even when she couldn't return the sentiment?

She was better with Behr. He was her happy, her support, her person. He reminded her that the weight of the world—and Helping Paws—

wasn't just on her shoulders. She'd always been better with Behr—right from the start.

Margo nosed between them, disrupting the kiss.

"Hey, Margo-girl." Ellery scrubbed behind her ears, under her chin.

Margo glanced at Behr as if checking if this intruder was okay.

"Margo! I'm offended. Who do you think knew you first? Not this guy." Ellery jutted her chin in Behr's direction.

"Ah, but she's mine now. You got knocked off the pedestal."

A smile erupted and grew as Ellery took in the picture before her. Margo completely in Behr's space. Behr completely at ease.

"You two look good together."

Behr's cheeks creased, the skin around his eyes crinkling. "Well, she's going to have to make room for another girl. No jealousy, okay?" He spoke to Margo, who dislodged herself from between them and settled behind with a sort of disgruntled, begrudging acceptance.

"You're a real dog whisperer, aren't you, Delgado?"

"That's right. Because I had the best of the best as a coach. I'll introduce you to her sometime. You'd like her."

At least this time, she *knew* he was teasing.

"Not sure how I feel about that," she dead-panned and layered her response with uncertainty. "I might be jealous meeting her."

Behr's chuckle was warm, as was his mouth as it hovered over hers, homing in for another kiss. "You should. She's pretty amazing."

Epilogue

Per the usual, Behr's parents' house was buzzing with people. Only this time, there was a particularly good reason for the chaos.

He and Ellery had opted for a casual, late-spring wedding on the shore of Mt. Vista Lake and a reception at the house.

Ellery was stunning in a simple white sheath dress that dipped low in the back. Behr knew the meaning of *sheath* because he'd heard his sisters discussing their approval of the style leading up to the wedding when they'd thought he wasn't paying attention. Like Dad, Behr was listening, even when they assumed he wasn't.

They'd gone with traditional vows, and Behr had fought back emotion when Ellery had clearly and lovingly repeated *in sickness and in health*, because to this day, he was aware of his inadequacies. Always would be. Though his new wife was continually reminding him of how strong and whole he was.

Behr had gained everything the day Ellery had arrived at his condo, upset with him for not showing up for training. God bless his sisters and Mom for signing him up for Margo.

Not that he planned to wax on about that. They needed no encouragement when it came to meddling.

"There you are." Ellery stepped onto the porch. Behr held out his arm, and she tucked into his right side since Margo occupied his left. "Your sisters just asked me if and when we're going to have kids."

"No. Seriously? What did you say?"

"I laughed."

"I'm glad you find them amusing. Otherwise you'd have gone running when you first met my family."

"You know I adore them. It actually made me think about how I could have missed all of this because I was so busy being a martyr for Ace's memory. As if it would somehow bring him back."

Behr squeezed her tighter. "Missing him today?"

Ellery nodded and blinked away moisture. "And Jake. I imagine he would have had quite the best man speech."

He would have teased and told stories and entertained and done his absolute best to embarrass Behr.

"Maybe it's better he's not here." Of course he didn't mean that. And of course Ellery knew that.

Marina, the kids and Kurt had come for the wedding—a bittersweet gift. And over the last year, Ellery's relationship with her parents had healed and grown. She'd leveled with them, sharing that when they'd lost Ace, she'd felt like she'd lost her parents, too. That they'd shut down with her in ways they maybe hadn't realized. That she missed them and hoped they could be more involved in each other's lives.

Her mom and dad had been devastated to hear that their actions—or lack thereof—had been hurting their daughter. Since then, they'd made more effort to support and reach out to Ellery. To visit Colorado. To talk with her on the phone weekly. Maybe Ace's death had broken them, but now they were figuring out how to live again. Just like Ellery had been doing. Just like Behr had been doing.

Fletcher stepped outside. He'd been an usher and was still wearing the dress pants and white button-down shirt, though his tie had been discarded somewhere.

Similar to his aunt, who'd tossed her strappy

heels to the side the minute they'd walked through the front door. Behr was pretty sure he'd seen his nieces taking turns modeling the shoes after Ellery had given them permission to do so. Truly, there wasn't a nook or cranny that his family didn't worm their way into.

"Fletcher! Don't you dare ask them right now." Desiree followed her son onto the porch and tried to drag him back into the house. Being that he'd shot up over the last year, her attempt to physically move him didn't pan out. "Sorry. You two were having a moment." Desiree gave her son a mom look that said, *Do not mess with me, child.* "Fletch is extremely apologetic for interrupting."

Fletcher wasn't fazed in the least. "No, I'm not."

Margo stood guard by Behr, warily studying the commotion, ready to provide assistance if needed. It was amazing how far Behr had come with her. How he'd gone from fearing her to needing her. She was the best support his family could have forced on him.

And she'd brought Ellery right to his door.

"Well, now I need to know." Ellery reached out to straighten Fletcher's collar. "What's going on?"

"Fletcher." Desiree's tone was deadly.

"What? I'm just going to say it, Mom. Aunt Ellery will be too curious if I don't."

Behr's chuckle was muted. Good to see that Fletcher, despite his uptick in height, was still an amusing, self-focused teenager. One with a good heart and good friends. One who'd changed in leaps and bounds since last summer.

"Mr. Bengal offered me a job at his construction firm this summer. It's entry-level stuff, and I really want to do it."

"That's great, Fletch!" Ellery beamed. The Bengals had turned out to be a great support for Helping Paws. They were committed to the cause, and Ellery and Behr had grown close to the other couple. Trip would be a great influence on the teenager.

Fletcher's attention switched to his Vans, which he'd worn for the ceremony because Ellery had declared that everyone should be comfortable.

"But I would have to live with you guys for a couple months," he mumbled and rushed over the explanation.

Desiree raised a slim brow. "See? This is why I told him not to bring this up—on your wedding day of all days! You can't just ask to live with *newlyweds* for the summer, Fletcher."

"And this has nothing to do with Raven,"

Behr interjected. "And everything to do with work, right?"

Fletcher's mouth hitched up on one side. "Uh, yeah. Right, right."

Amusement threaded through the adults. He'd been texting and talking to Raven since last summer. Absolutely no one believed Fletcher wanted to live with them because of a job. Or at least not *just* because of a job.

"We'll discuss it, Fletch." Ellery hugged Desiree, likely whispering some assurance in her ear that it was okay for Fletcher to ask—even on their wedding day.

Alessandra poked her head onto the porch. "I need you two." She pointed at Behr and Ellery. "Gotta cut the cake." She made a snipping motion.

"I'm not sure who put you in charge of everything, Less. Pretty sure we can cut the cake whenever we want."

"Not if you two hope to get out of here anytime before midnight." It was the worst when Alessandra was right. "And your *wife* put me in charge, Behr-Behr."

Not exactly true. Alessandra had taken over in terms of running the reception on a schedule, and Ellery had let her, since her strategy for the evening was to enjoy herself and every moment with their friends and family. Which meant Behr should probably thank Alessandra for her intrusion, but once again, he didn't plan to do that.

His *oldest* sister needed no encouragement when it came to overstepping.

"We'll be in in a sec." He inclined his head to concede Alessandra's win and earned a triumphant grin from her.

Desiree and Fletcher followed Alessandra inside, Desiree giving Fletcher an earful about etiquette and what was *proper*.

Ellery turned to Behr. "Can't say I expected that conversation. Guess it's my turn to apologize for an intrusive family. Don't feel any pressure with Fletcher. We can pray about it and absolutely say no. He'll be fine."

Behr was certain he would be. But he also knew Ellery *really* loved her nephew. And her sister-in-law. And his whole over-the-top family. She would enjoy having Fletcher around, even if he was barely around.

"I don't mind the idea of him staying with us this summer. He'll be so busy between work and Raven that we'll probably never see him anyway."

"I had that same thought!"

"In fact… I kind of like it. Makes me feel like I'm doing something for the Jakes and the

Aces. The dads who didn't get to come home and raise their kids."

Ellery's eyes glistened. "I can't think of a better role model for Fletcher than you."

"Think pretty highly of me, do you?"

"Yep." She used his charcoal tie to tug him close and press a kiss to his cheek. Like a good boy, Behr had left his tie on even though it was itching to be loosened. Ellery had been the least demanding and most relaxed bride ever, therefore Behr wasn't going to fuss about a thing.

"I think the same about you." Behr wrapped his wife into a hug, pressing a kiss just below her ear, earning a shiver. "Did I mention you're stunning? Today. Always." When she'd walked toward him on the small beach, the oxygen in Behr's lungs had evaporated. Ellery was a vision. She was achingly beautiful on the outside and the inside. "You're the best thing that's ever happened to me times a thousand, Ellery Watson Delgado."

He felt her smile and her love as she nestled against him like she never planned to let go. "Same, kid. Same."

* * * * *

*If you enjoyed this K-9 Companions book,
be sure to look for* Her Easter Prayer
by New York Times *bestselling author
Lee Tobin McClain,
available April 2022 wherever
Love Inspired books are sold!*

Dear Reader,

Thank you for joining me in a new fictional town in Colorado. It's a privilege to share Ellery and Behr's story. It's also a privilege to experience the freedoms we do in America. I'd like to thank the many veterans and their families who have served our country. Thank you, thank you for your countless sacrifices.

While Behr perceives his "weakness" as exactly that, everyone around him is able to see his strength and perseverance. I believe it so often happens that way in our own lives. We can be so hard on ourselves and feel so alone in our battles. Whatever you are going through—whatever your present "weakness"—may you find comfort and confidence with God as your strength and support.

Many readers have helped to name characters or have weighed in online over various stages of book plotting. Thank you for that! It's a joy to interact with you all. I hang out at Facebook.com/JillLynnAuthor and Instagram.com/JillLynnAuthor. I also share updates and giveaways in my newsletter. Sign up is at Jill-Lynn.com/news.

Blessings!
Jill Lynn

Get 4 FREE REWARDS!

We'll send you 2 FREE Books plus 2 FREE Mystery Gifts.

FREE Value Over **$20**

Both the **Love Inspired®** and **Love Inspired® Suspense** series feature compelling novels filled with inspirational romance, faith, forgiveness, and hope.

YES! Please send me 2 FREE novels from the Love Inspired or Love Inspired Suspense series and my 2 FREE gifts (gifts are worth about $10 retail). After receiving them, if I don't wish to receive any more books, I can return the shipping statement marked "cancel." If I don't cancel, I will receive 6 brand-new Love Inspired Larger-Print books or Love Inspired Suspense Larger-Print books every month and be billed just $5.99 each in the U.S. or $6.24 each in Canada. That is a savings of at least 17% off the cover price. It's quite a bargain! Shipping and handling is just 50¢ per book in the U.S. and $1.25 per book in Canada.* I understand that accepting the 2 free books and gifts places me under no obligation to buy anything. I can always return a shipment and cancel at any time. The free books and gifts are mine to keep no matter what I decide.

Choose one:
☐ **Love Inspired**
Larger-Print
(122/322 IDN GNWC)

☐ **Love Inspired Suspense**
Larger-Print
(107/307 IDN GNWN)

Name (please print)

Address
Apt. #

City
State/Province
Zip/Postal Code

Email: Please check this box ☐ if you would like to receive newsletters and promotional emails from Harlequin Enterprises ULC and its affiliates. You can unsubscribe anytime.

Mail to the Harlequin Reader Service:
IN U.S.A.: P.O. Box 1341, Buffalo, NY 14240-8531
IN CANADA: P.O. Box 603, Fort Erie, Ontario L2A 5X3

Want to try 2 free books from another series? Call 1-800-873-8635 or visit www.ReaderService.com.

*Terms and prices subject to change without notice. Prices do not include sales taxes, which will be charged (if applicable) based on your state or country of residence. Canadian residents will be charged applicable taxes. Offer not valid in Quebec. This offer is limited to one order per household. Books received may not be as shown. Not valid for current subscribers to the Love Inspired or Love Inspired Suspense series. All orders subject to approval. Credit or debit balances in a customer's account(s) may be offset by any other outstanding balance owed by or to the customer. Please allow 4 to 6 weeks for delivery. Offer available while quantities last.

Your Privacy—Your information is being collected by Harlequin Enterprises ULC, operating as Harlequin Reader Service. For a complete summary of the information we collect, how we use this information and to whom it is disclosed, please visit our privacy notice located at corporate.harlequin.com/privacy-notice. From time to time we may also exchange your personal information with reputable third parties. If you wish to opt out of this sharing of your personal information, please visit readerservice.com/consumerchoice or call 1-800-873-8635. **Notice to California Residents**—Under California law, you have specific rights to control and access your data. For more information on these rights and how to exercise them, visit corporate.harlequin.com/california-privacy.

LIRLIS22

Get 4 FREE REWARDS!

We'll send you 2 FREE Books plus 2 FREE Mystery Gifts.

FREE
Value Over
$20

Both the **Harlequin® Special Edition** and **Harlequin® Heartwarming™** series feature compelling novels filled with stories of love and strength where the bonds of friendship, family and community unite.

YES! Please send me 2 FREE novels from the Harlequin Special Edition or Harlequin Heartwarming series and my 2 FREE gifts (gifts are worth about $10 retail). After receiving them, if I don't wish to receive any more books, I can return the shipping statement marked "cancel." If I don't cancel, I will receive 6 brand-new Harlequin Special Edition books every month and be billed just $4.99 each in the U.S or $5.74 each in Canada, a savings of at least 17% off the cover price or 4 brand-new Harlequin Heartwarming Larger-Print books every month and be billed just $5.74 each in the U.S. or $6.24 each in Canada, a savings of at least 21% off the cover price. It's quite a bargain! Shipping and handling is just 50¢ per book in the U.S. and $1.25 per book in Canada.* I understand that accepting the 2 free books and gifts places me under no obligation to buy anything. I can always return a shipment and cancel at any time. The free books and gifts are mine to keep no matter what I decide.

Choose one: ☐ **Harlequin Special Edition**
(235/335 HDN GNMP)   ☐ **Harlequin Heartwarming**
Larger-Print
(161/361 HDN GNPZ)

Name (please print)

Address   Apt. #

City   State/Province   Zip/Postal Code

Email: Please check this box ☐ if you would like to receive newsletters and promotional emails from Harlequin Enterprises ULC and its affiliates. You can unsubscribe anytime.

Mail to the **Harlequin Reader Service:**
IN U.S.A.: P.O. Box 1341, Buffalo, NY 14240-8531
IN CANADA: P.O. Box 603, Fort Erie, Ontario L2A 5X3

Want to try 2 free books from another series? Call 1-800-873-8635 or visit www.ReaderService.com.

*Terms and prices subject to change without notice. Prices do not include sales taxes, which will be charged (if applicable) based on your state or country of residence. Canadian residents will be charged applicable taxes. Offer not valid in Quebec. This offer is limited to one order per household. Books received may not be as shown. Not valid for current subscribers to the Harlequin Special Edition or Harlequin Heartwarming series. All orders subject to approval. Credit or debit balances in a customer's account(s) may be offset by any other outstanding balance owed by or to the customer. Please allow 4 to 6 weeks for delivery. Offer available while quantities last.

Your Privacy—Your information is being collected by Harlequin Enterprises ULC, operating as Harlequin Reader Service. For a complete summary of the information we collect, how we use this information and to whom it is disclosed, please visit our privacy notice located at corporate.harlequin.com/privacy-notice. From time to time we may also exchange your personal information with reputable third parties. If you wish to opt out of this sharing of your personal information, please visit readerservice.com/consumerchoice or call 1-800-873-8635. **Notice to California Residents**—Under California law, you have specific rights to control and access your data. For more information on these rights and how to exercise them, visit corporate.harlequin.com/california-privacy.

HSEHW22

COUNTRY LEGACY COLLECTION

19 FREE BOOKS IN ALL!

Cowboys, adventure and romance await you in this new collection! Enjoy superb reading all year long with books by bestselling authors like Diana Palmer, Sasha Summers and Marie Ferrarella!

YES! Please send me the **Country Legacy Collection!** This collection begins with 3 FREE books and 2 FREE gifts in the first shipment. Along with my 3 free books, I'll also get 3 more books from the **Country Legacy Collection**, which I may either return and owe nothing or keep for the low price of $24.60 U.S./$28.12 CDN each plus $2.99 U.S./$7.49 CDN for shipping and handling per shipment*. If I decide to continue, about once a month for 8 months, I will get 6 or 7 more books but will only pay for 4. That means 2 or 3 books in every shipment will be FREE! If I decide to keep the entire collection, I'll have paid for only 32 books because 19 are FREE! I understand that accepting the 3 free books and gifts places me under no obligation to buy anything. I can always return a shipment and cancel at any time. My free books and gifts are mine to keep no matter what I decide.

☐ 275 HCK 1939   ☐ 475 HCK 1939

Name (please print)

Address   Apt. #

City   State/Province   Zip/Postal Code

Mail to the Harlequin Reader Service:
IN U.S.A.: P.O. Box 1341, Buffalo, NY 14240-8571
IN CANADA: P.O. Box 603, Fort Erie, Ontario L2A 5X3

*Terms and prices subject to change without notice. Prices do not include sales taxes, which will be charged (if applicable) based on your state or country of residence. Canadian residents will be charged applicable taxes. Offer not valid in Quebec. All orders subject to approval. Credit or debit balances in a customer's account(s) may be offset by any other outstanding balance owed by or to the customer. Please allow 3 to 4 weeks for delivery. Offer available while quantities last. © 2021 Harlequin Enterprises ULC ® and ™ are trademarks owned by Harlequin Enterprises ULC.

Your Privacy—Your information is being collected by Harlequin Enterprises ULC, operating as Harlequin Reader Service. To see how we collect and use this information visit https://corporate.harlequin.com/privacy-notice. From time to time we may also exchange your personal information with reputable third parties. If you wish to opt out of this sharing of your personal information, please visit www.readerservice.com/consumerschoice or call 1-800-873-8635. Notice to California Residents—Under California law, you have specific rights to control and access your data. For more information visit https://corporate.harlequin.com/california-privacy.

50BOOKCL22

COMING NEXT MONTH FROM
Love Inspired

MISTAKEN FOR HIS AMISH BRIDE
North Country Amish • by Patricia Davids

Traveling to Maine to search for family, Mari Kemp is injured in an accident—and ends up with amnesia. Mistakenly believing she's the fiancée he's been corresponding with, Asher Fisher will do anything to help Mari recover her memories. But can he remember the past in time to see their future?

THE AMISH ANIMAL DOCTOR
by Patrice Lewis

Veterinarian Abigail Mast returns to her Amish community to care for her ailing mother and must pick between her career and the Amish life. Her handsome neighbor Benjamin Troyer isn't making the decision any easier. An impossible choice could lead to her greatest reward...

HER EASTER PRAYER
K-9 Companions • by Lee Tobin McClain

To heal from a past tragedy, Emily Carver and service dog Lady have devoted themselves to teaching children—including handyman Dev McCarthy's troubled son. But Dev's struggles with reading might need their help more. Can they learn to trust each other and write a happy ending to their story?

KEEPING THEM SAFE
Sundown Valley • by Linda Goodnight

Feeling honor bound to help others, rancher Bowie Trudeau is instantly drawn to former best friend Sage Walker—and her young niece and nephew—when she returns thirteen years later. Certain she'll leave again, Bowie's determined to not get attached. But this little family might just show him the true meaning of home...

A FOSTER MOTHER'S PROMISE
Kendrick Creek • by Ruth Logan Herne

Opening her heart and home to children in need is Carly Bradley's goal in life. But when she can't get through to a troubled little girl in her care, she turns to gruff new neighbor Mike Morris. Closed off after a tragic past, Mike might discover happiness next door...

AN ALASKAN SECRET
Home to Hearts Bay • by Heidi McCahan

Wildlife biologist Asher Hale never expected returning home to Hearts Bay, Alaska, would put him face-to-face with his ex Tess Madden—or that she would be his son's second-grade teacher. Their love starts to rekindle, but as buried memories come to light, could their second chance be ruined forever?

LOOK FOR THESE AND OTHER LOVE INSPIRED BOOKS WHEREVER BOOKS ARE SOLD, INCLUDING MOST BOOKSTORES, SUPERMARKETS, DISCOUNT STORES AND DRUGSTORES.

LICNM0222